MEMergence

The HuMEM Series: Book One

BY
KATE DONNELLY

COPYRIGHT©2014KATEDONNELLY

Reproducing this book without permission from the author or the publisher is an infringement of its copyright. This book is a work of fiction. The names characters, places, and incidents are products of the author's imagination and are not to be construed as real. Any resemblance to any actual events or persons, living or dead, locale or organizations is entirely coincidental.

Book Cover by Steven J. Catizone -Elance

DEDICATION

I dedicate this book to my Husband and Daughter who believe in me. Thank you so much for your encouragement and insistence that I continue writing this story. It has been a challenging and rewarding endeavor!

PROLOGUE

I wake and hear screaming—sharp, piercing screams—guttural groans. I turn to my right to see a young woman looking at me, begging me to help her. I try to get up, but my arms and legs are secured to a gurney. Then I realize, I too am in pain—horrible agonizing pain. How did this happen?

The room is crowded with people in scrubs, shouting numbers, attaching things to me everywhere. I try to pull free, but they are holding me down. I want to help this girl.

"Let me go!" I shout. "I need to get up!" My pain is too great. "Please," I cry, "help her."

The girl's back arches and she struggles to free herself, all the while screaming; she looks at me with bewilderment. Her mouth moves as if she is saying something. It is heart wrenching. Then someone steps between us and I feel a prick in my arm and I relax. My eyes start to close, but not before I see the young woman has also stopped struggling; she looks terrified.

CHAPTER 1

Three Months Earlier

Armed with determination and self-loathing, I have discovered what it is like to be fifty-five and in great shape. I swim laps every morning, even though the pool at the "Y" is clouded with a haze of chlorine that floats above the heated water. My nose burns at the end of a 45-minute exposure to its noxious fumes. However, my joints had been hurting from the extra fifty pounds that I had been lugging around with me every day and swimming allows me to exercise without pain. Now that I am forty pounds lighter, I have been using the treadmill and lifting weights.

I recently cut my shoulder-length hair and let it fall naturally into complete disarray. I have a lot of thick, coarse, mousey, brown hair with natural blonde streaks that is slowly turning white at the roots. As the weight has come off, it's revealed more wrinkles, especially around my narrow-set, slate blue eyes and at the corners of my smile. And my neck is falling—where will it go?

Looking around the gym, I see young hunks lifting

weights and think again about the unfairness of life. Why do we have to age at all? Here are gorgeous male specimens with buff bodies and in twenty or thirty years, they could be pot-bellied, shoulder-slouching, self-absorbed, middle age Romeos taking Viagra and chasing younger women—or men—in a futile attempt to pretend their lives aren't hurdling toward a pointless end.

I giggle to myself as I gaze over all this male eye candy, noticing my friend Tess is waving wildly for me to join her for a water break. Tess is aging gracefully and I am always comparing myself to her. Her mouth doesn't turn down, nor do her knees look like they are bowing to the ground. She has firm breasts and her stomach is flat. She is two years older than me, but has no husband and no children; I have both and feel this justifies my extra pounds. I am married and have an adult daughter and one granddaughter.

"Beautiful, aren't they?" Tess exclaims, resting her elbow on the counter, her chin in her hand.

"What I wouldn't give to be young and have their attention! Can you imagine all that muscle under your hands?"

"Hey, Preston isn't anything to sneeze at. He takes good care of himself. You should be happy to have such a good looking husband." She says.

I look at her for a long minute. Am I imagining things or is it possible she has a thing for my husband? She never seems to want to come over when he is home.

"Yeah, he has great legs, flat abs, and the rest of him is pretty muscular in an older dude sort of way. Just wish he had one muscle that worked better."

Tess raised her eyebrows. "Really? Huh."

Then she changes the subject. "Come on Opal," she begs, starting in again where our conversation had ended during our last water break. "You are so much smarter than me."

"No way!" I say. "I wouldn't last two seconds with all those people staring at me." The thought of going on television scares me.

"You could be a millionaire!" Tess says, eyes open wide. "One million dollars. One million! Where would you ever get that much money? You...you could go to Switzerland, to that clinic you saw advertised in that magazine." She giggles. "Remember?"

I shake my head and laugh.

"Yeah, Star Genesis, the total body renewal. What a crock!"

"Opal, you are the smartest person I know. You know more trivia than Alex Trebek!" She laughs. "Maybe you could write questions for Jeopardy."

"Is that a job?" I ask.

She looks at me wide-eyed. "Someone has to come up

with all that stuff. Look," she says. "I already went ahead and ....um... signed you up for the show. Last month."

She doesn't look up, keeping her eyes on her hands. "I got a response and you have been accepted to show up the first week in February. That's like eight months away!"

She smiles hopefully, but I am already headed for the door.

How dare she! "Well, you have fun with that!" I throw over my shoulder shouting as I make my escape for the locker room. I don't bother to shower, throwing on my sundress, stuffing everything into my gym bag, and I am out the door before she can catch me. My phone is ringing as I drive out of the parking lot. It is Tess, so I just let it ring. I sniff at my shoulder; it smells like chlorine.

The ringtone on my phone announces that my daughter is calling, so I answer.

"Sorry to bother you, Mom," she shouts over the screaming voice of my four-year-old granddaughter, "but can you swing by the market and pick up a few things for me? My car had a flat this morning."

She reads off her list. "I will try to remember it all. Let's see there are nine things you needed?" I ask. Every chance I get, I preform mental exercises to boost my memory.

Shopping complete, I hand Laura the groceries and pick up my darling grandchild, Lucy. Her hair has soft strawberry-blonde ringlets that bounce up and down, as she does. I stroke her soft skin and covet the silky smooth texture. Her eyes capture mine and I see unconditional acceptance.

"Do you have gum?" she asks, batting the eyelashes of her big blue eyes.

"You minx!" I laugh at her as I dig through my purse looking for gum.

"I can't stay long," I say. "I have to get back to the house before your dad. He wants to go looking for a new putter and is taking me out to dinner."

Laura hands me a glass of ice water. "You can at least take a load off for a little while and sit. I must say, that exercising is doing wonders. How many dress sizes have you dropped?"

"Thanks," I accept the water. "Three. I am now down to a size ten."

Laura has finally lost her baby weight and is as thin as she was before the birth of Lucy. Her hair is shoulder length and a beautiful shade of brown. Her eyes are yellow green and she is quickly reading through an article in a magazine that I had given to her last week.

"Just now scanning the ad?" I say.

"Sorry," she smiles with chagrin. "You know what my days are like with a four-year-old."

You have two "Mother's-Days-Out a week," I say

accusingly.

"Okay, I forgot." She looks back at the article. "This doesn't sound right. They are using stem cells to change the skin texture. Where do they get the stem cells?" She wrinkles her nose. "I mean, they have to come from a person don't they? It isn't like they can use stem cells from animals!" Laura laughs.

"Oh my gosh," she says, "what if they are using stem cells from pigs? Pigs have nice skin don't they? Nice pinkish skin with long hair sticking out around their snouts? Isn't it true that some pig organs are used in people?" She teases.

"I don't believe they would use stem cells from animals on people." I say seriously, but still smiling at Laura's joke.

"You aren't seriously considering having any work done there, are you?" Laura stops laughing. "Surely you will do more checking around before you decide to turn yourself over to some *quack*."

"I don't think they are quacks." I explain. "This is a serious clinic involved in serious research. I look at her intently. "Are you really afraid for me or do you just not want me to be prettier than you?"

She chuckles. "Mom, you are beautiful just the way you are, but if you aren't happy with yourself, then by all means take every opportunity that comes your way."

Laura puts her arm around my shoulder. "I love you,

Mom. You have taken care of everybody with no care for yourself...for years. You deserve to take time to make yourself happy. And if this is what will make you happy, then go for it!

Her eyes light up. "Switzerland sounds cool! Bring me back some chocolate!"

"More gum?" Lucy croons, leaning on my knees shaking her head up and down.

Guess she swallowed the last piece.

"No more gum. All gone," I tell her and give her a big hug.

"It isn't a done deal. I'm just thinking about it. It has always been a desire of mine to look in the mirror and see a beautiful dewy complexion with tight pores and even skin tone."

I sigh wistfully, thinking I sound like a commercial. "Maybe I'm just fooling myself. It may not change anything." I reach out and touch the dark circles under my daughter's eyes. "You look tired, Laura. Are you feeling okay?"

She stretches. "Yeah, I just get tired easily. I've cut back to one cup of coffee a day, so I think I need more caffeine. I've been drinking more green tea."

"I worry about you. You need to get out more with friends. Dad and I will watch Lucy." I say. "Ever since Chad died, you've kept to yourself."

"Mom, don't start." She rolls her eyes. "I just haven't

met anyone I like. Besides, I'm content with my life. The insurance left me with enough money to live until Lucy is in school full-time. I'll get a job and get out more then."

I kiss Lucy and Laura and leave for home.

CHAPTER 2

As I arrive home, I really regret not showering at the gym. I slip into the bathroom for a quick one before Preston and I go to dinner and ponder the possibility of going to Switzerland. I didn't really let on to Tess that I am seriously considering the trip. She wants to go along, but I'm looking forward to the week of peace and quiet during recovery—there's nothing peaceful or quiet about spending time with Tess.

I should take my guitar and write some songs while I'm there. I miss the healing and self-expression that comes with song writing. There is so much about life I can't express by talking. I used to spend hours just singing about what I was feeling. I actually sold a couple of songs that have become hits, when I was younger. Occasionally, I'll hear one of my songs on the radio and it's still a thrill.

Few people understand what it's like to get older, until it happens to them. When I think about the fact that the man I'm married to will soon be seventy, it is a difficult place to be. Then the realization that I am only a few years from turning sixty myself hits hard. I may only live for another ten or fifteen years. Maybe I'll live twenty extra years if I take care and watch my weight.

What if my husband dies before I turn sixty-two? I won't be able to live on his social security or pension until I'm age eligible. I will have to go to work. What would I do? Preston never wanted me to work outside the home; surely, he has considered this possibility. I should talk to him about this.

People get so used to trying to please others, that sometimes they get lost. That's me. I feel lost and I'm trying to find my way back to myself. I feel like I am still young inside. But when I get physical, my body is far older than my soul.

There is so much I haven't experienced in this life, and time is running out. I would love to find the Fountain of Youth and take a nice big gulp. Even though that isn't possible, I don't have to be content with getting older—I want do everything I can to keep myself healthy and looking younger, starting with this trip to Switzerland.

Preston arrives home two hours later than he had planned. He stopped by the golf shop and bought his new club on the way home, met some buddies, and had a bite to eat. It irritates me that he doesn't have the decency to phone and let me know of his changed plans.

I make myself an egg on toast with steamed spinach

and, now that I've made my decision, I try to work up the courage to talk to him about the clinic.

Our marriage has always been like this—I have never been comfortable with speaking my mind or taking action that Preston might disapprove of. Probably because he always seems to think that what I want is trivial or frivolous; he is constantly insisting that I look at the "bigger plan?" Is it important to buy myself a new purse when the money can be put to better use? Do I really need to take a pottery class when I won't be able to use all the things I will make? Why pay for the expensive brand when the cheaper kind works the same? Of course, *he* always wears the best, *he* buys the best, and *he* never skimps when it comes to himself.

He's always had this way of making me feel like I am living off charity. Apparently raising our child, keeping his house, cooking his meals, doing his laundry, and anything else he asks of me counts for nothing!

Sometimes, I wonder if Preston's loss of interest in our relationship is because I'm always so complacent. I am not happy, but I never stand up for myself. I haven't been happy for several years and I know he isn't happy either.

It has been three years since he has kissed me with any passion, and just as long since we have had sex. I've lost weight, dyed my hair, and once again taken up song writing in an effort to make myself more interesting and attract his attention. I wear provocative tops letting my cleavage show and I flirt with him. Sometimes he smiles at me and flirts back, but that's as far as it ever goes.

My heart is aching for his touch, but fear of rejection keeps me from saying anything. Because I worry that he will say something that will devastate me, I won't let a more serious discussion develop about his apparent lack of libido. He would certainly never bring it up and his lack of concern for my feelings just adds to my sadness and the seemingly insurmountable tension between us.

Thirty-five years of marriage and Preston's constant barrage of manipulations has turned me into a meek submissive. I can't really blame him; I think he wants a wife who will stand up to his manipulative ways and be an equal in this partnership. But then, maybe he won't like it and will leave. The thought is always in the back of my mind; can I survive on my own? I don't think so.

Well, it is now or never. I need to stake a claim in my own life and prove to myself that I can be independent and suck up life on my own.

I brace my disillusioned heart and march myself into the den to speak with my husband.

"Sorry," he says, looking up from the newspaper he is reading. "I should have called you, but I left my Blackberry at the office."

"I guess they don't have phones at the club where you ate, huh?"

"I have no excuses." He looks crestfallen.

Has he always used this look to make me feel guilty? I'm starting to realize he has been using this manipulation technique our entire marriage. And I always give in, because I can't stand to hurt him or have him displeased with me.

"Never mind," I say. "I do have something I want to tell you. I am considering a trip to Switzerland, to visit a clinic."

"A what?" he interrupts.

"Let me finish," I say. "I have my own money and this is what I want to do. I have always wanted to have a beautiful complexion and the clinic performs an experimental procedure that takes years off one's appearance; I want to do this."

"What do you mean you have your own money?" he asks.

I sigh. It's *always* about the money. "I sold one of Mother's old lithographs and it brought in enough money for me to make this trip and have the treatment."

"But we can take a vacation together with that money," he says. "We want to go to Guatemala to visit my brother."

"Have you always been this way?" I look at him incredulously. "You want to go see your brother; I want to do this and that is what I am going to do! If you wanted the money for a vacation to Guatemala, why did you spend money on that expensive golf club?"

I'm proud of myself for standing up to him. I am tired of putting away my desires and ideas because of his overwhelming need to be in control.

"Are you serious?" he began mocking me. "You can't really be serious. Do you think they can turn back the clock or something? Why can't you be content with being your age and stop all this nonsense?"

"Why did you stop making love to me?" I decide that rejection or not, I am on a pathway to enlightenment that may lead to my demise, but the freedom to express myself lights my determination.

He shrugs his shoulders. "You don't want to get into this," he says.

"Yes, I do. Don't you think it strange that we haven't talked about this in three years?" I search his face for truth. "Please, tell me." I look down at myself. "I know I'm not much to look at, but I am working on it. I thought maybe if I could change my skin texture, or have my eyes done, you would find me attractive again."

He turns away. "I just don't have any desire to have sex."

"A doctor could help us," I say. "They have medicine for that."

He scowls. "I don't want medicine. I don't want to make love to you."

"So, it *is* the way I look? It *is* my age!"

I walk out of the room to evade the hostility I see in his eyes. He's confirmed my worst fears; he isn't interested in me anymore.

"Opal," he calls after me. "Please, don't spend that money foolishly."

"It only seems foolish to you, Preston!" I yell back into the other room. My voice is bitter and my expression is flat. "Only to you," I finish in a whisper

Preston sleeps in the guest room and I cry myself to sleep. I think about going to him and apologizing. After all, I tell myself, he has always taken care of you. Don't you owe him loyalty?

Loyalty? What am I, a housebroken dog? And what about his loyalty to me? That loyalty isn't only about keeping himself for me physically, but also about his respecting me emotionally and mentally. I've never disagreed with him about anything. I've kept his house, washed his clothes, made his meals and been his companion. When he wanted me to quit my job, I stayed home with Laura. I shopped where he thought I should, when he said it was okay, and didn't argue.

I need to find pride in myself again. I need to make myself happy and be content with who I am. I have hidden so long in the stereotypes that life prepared for me that I've lost Opal. I see myself as Daughter, Wife, Mother, and Grandmother. And I am comfortable with those roles, but isn't my substance greater than all of that? I know I could do anything I want if given the chance. To think that I waited until I was fifty-five to break into my own! Gumption! That's what I lack. That's probably why Preston has no respect for me.

Over the next few months, I apply to the program and make arrangements to travel at the end of July, while Preston tries several more times to talk me out of going. I won't entertain doubt, nor let a negative thought take hold in my mind. I am determined to get on a plane and change my life by doing what I want to do.

The clinic calls a month before departure and tells me to visit a Dr. Sylvia Rushing in Atlanta, GA. where she will take blood samples and prepare the formula for the patients who are chosen for the procedure. During my visit, she tells me they have to mix the nanites with my DNA before the procedure to insure a stable environment and that the stem cells will perform, whatever that means.

It's been a month since my trip to Atlanta, and I've received my final acceptance into the program. I leave for the airport in Nashville at 8:00 a.m. and Preston refuses to accompany me, so Tess does the honors. She hands me a gift bag and gives me a big hug.

"Don't you worry about any little thing. I'm sure the doctor will have everything under control." She looks around at the crowded entrance. "Guess security won't let me go with you to the gate, unless I purchase a ticket, so I'll say goodbye here. I hope you enjoy your time in Switzerland. You want me to check on Preston?"

"Thank you for the gift," I said hugging her back. "I'll email you and let you know everything. Preston is a big boy; he can take care of himself. Besides, I'll only be gone a week at most."

I pull my bag up to the counter and after it is out of sight on the conveyor belt, I step up to the security line and wait for my turn at the metal detector. I find the gate I need and open Tess' gift. There is a book, some magazines, a journal, and a string bikini. I laugh out loud. She'd promised to buy me one if I lost fifty pounds. I still have seven to go, but I won't be caught dead in this little thing. It is a size small! Tess is a good friend and always knows how to make me laugh.

The flight is long and tedious, even in First Class with room to move around. The meal isn't too bad, but I am more tired than hungry. All the stress Preston has put me under, with his unwillingness to compromise this one time for something I want to do, has worn me out. I hope that I will find some time of peace while I'm at the spa.

I pick up my luggage and walk through immigration in

Switzerland. As I near the exit, I spot a woman holding a sign for the Genesis Spa and walk her way. She is stunningly beautiful. The man standing next to her leans down to say something in her ear. He too is a looker, but there is something about her skin that draws my attention. She is radiant. Her hair is long, dark and shiny with a hint of waves. Her teeth are white and her eyes have a light that shows she is full of life. Wow! If this is what the Spa does, I am glad to be chosen to participate.

I approach the two of them.

"Hello, I'm headed to the Spa." I wait for her to turn her eyes to me.

"Yes," Her voice is magical. "Are you Opal Sanders?"

"That's correct." I hand her my written invitation.

"Lonnie will load your bags and you can climb inside and sit down. We will leave in approximately twenty minutes." She glances at her watch. Then she looks at me and smiles. "I'm Zoe."

I shake her hand, turning it over and admiring her skin. "You are beautiful."

"Thank you, Mrs. Sanders. That is kind of you." She smiles bigger.

The ride to the Spa takes several hours. It seems we have landed in Zurich, but the Spa is on the Mountain by St. Gallen. It is 2:00 a.m. when I'm shown to my room and climb into bed.

The next morning I awake to the insistent knocking at my door. A nurse walks in and introduces herself as Heike, Dr.Rushing's assistant. She is here to check my vitals and take a few more blood samples.

After breakfast, I have the day to myself and partake in all that the Spa has to offer. Heike schedules a deep-tissue massage and a gentle stretching class for me in the afternoon. I have permission to eat all three meals today, but I am to have nothing after 7:00 pm tonight. She informs me that I can have water to rinse my mouth after brushing, but I'm not to swallow. She also states that this is a medical procedure and that I will be put under anesthesia like an operation.

For some reason, that sets my nerves on edge. I hadn't realized I would go under anesthesia. I don't know why I thought it would be a simple procedure like putting a topical lotion on my skin. They plan to introduce the nanites in a DNA/stem cell mixture that will be injected under my skin. Why hadn't I asked about this before?

I go to the dining room and eat a breakfast of muesli and fruit. Then come back to my room and email Preston, Laura, and Tess, letting them know I have arrived safely.

I walk in the beautiful gardens before heading to lunch where I sit with several other women who are also having the same procedure. They are excited; two have their operations scheduled before my own. I hope that that will mean Dr. Rushing will be in a groove and whizz right into my procedure without any problems.

I'm plagued by doubts throughout the day and I struggle to get my emotions under control. This is really happening and the more I try to relax, the more anxious I get; I am actually shaking. I return to the garden outside, trying to settle my nerves through deep breathing. If I don't get a hold on my feelings, I am headed for a panic attack.

By the time dusk comes to the mountain, I am feeling relaxed and tired. I've finally brought my thoughts and emotions through the valley of despair and I am ready to face tomorrow's procedure with some enthusiasm.

CHAPTER 3

I wake and hear screaming—sharp, piercing screams—guttural groans. I turn to my right to see a young woman looking at me, begging me to help her. I try to get up, but my arms and legs are secured to a gurney. Then I realize, I too am in pain—horrible agonizing pain. How did this happen?

The room is crowded with people in scrubs, shouting numbers, attaching things to me everywhere. I try to pull free, but they are holding me down. I want to help this girl.

"Let me go!" I shout. "I need to get up!" My pain is too great. "Please," I cry, "help her."

The girl's back arches and she struggles to free herself, all the while screaming; she looks at me with bewilderment. Her mouth moves as if she is saying something. It is heart wrenching. Then someone steps between us and I feel a prick in my arm and I relax. My eyes start to close, but not before I see the young woman has also stopped struggling; she looks terrified.

When this happens again, I wonder if I am dreaming. Why am I in so much pain if I am only having the simple skin procedure? My insides feel like they are being ripped apart. I struggle to breathe, as trembling neck spasms cause my head to slam repeatedly against the table. Someone straps my forehead to hold it in place and I strive to turn my head to catch a glimpse of the young woman I saw earlier.

Where was she? Are we victims of an earthquake, a war, or a natural disaster? These are the thoughts that flood my mind as I fall in and out of consciousness, always feeling a prick in my arm shortly before fading out again.

I finally wake up without pain and find myself back in my room. The light is bright and I know it must be nearing noon. I stretch my arms by my sides and sigh, but I am unable to lift my hands. My face is still covered in bandages and I soon realize I am peeking out of eyeholes. The nurse leans over me so I can see her.

"Don't move too much," she says. "You have recently returned from surgery and I don't want you to jostle the bandages."

"Bandages? Surgery? No one said anything about bandages." I try to get up. "What's happened?" My voice is muffled.

"Well," she smiles sweetly. "There were some complications, but I'm sure you are going to love the final results."

"What has happened? Please, am I dying? I feel so

dizzy."

I lay back and my eyes close. Then from somewhere, I gain strength and start in again. "When will the bandages come off?" I slur my words and my voice sounds raspy. "Can I talk to the doctor? Why are my hands still tied to the bed?" My voice creaks to a higher pitch. "I demand to be let up!" I pull at the straps binding my arms and kick my legs.

She steps closer to my bed and, as I feel the familiar prick of a needle, I begin to fade into oblivion, again.

My head aches when I come to, and I see the young woman across from me again. I am back in the surgery room and I am covered in blood. It seems to be coming from my mouth. The doctor is speaking to me.

"Opal, look at me!" She orders. "Spit into my hand, you have something in your mouth. I don't want you to choke."

I try to grasp her words, but none of it makes any sense. She leans me forward and puts a metal bowl in front of my face. Obediently I spit. My mouth is strange and my tongue captures the offending objects and ejects them into the bowl. One by one, they make a clunking sound. My tongue takes a feel around my mouth and feels nothing....no teeth. What is happening to me? Blood everywhere! My God, am I dying?

I look towards the young woman as she screams obscenities. Her eyes are filled with fear. She too is covered in blood. We must have been in the same disaster? Something about her looks familiar. Do I know her? I must have seen her in the dining room or spa.

When I wake again, I feel strange, but, the bandages are gone and my arms are free. My hair is in my face and I reach up to move the offending locks. I can see them; golden like the sun and very long. My hair? I notice slender hands and the lithe arms to which they are attached. Can it be possible that I was in a coma so long that I have lost weight? How many days would I have been out and not eating to lose so much weight? I wiggle my fingers and they obey, so it must be my arm.

The nurse nears my bed.

"Can I have a glass of water?" I hear my voice. It sounds different, lighter and higher pitched than I remember.

She lifts the straw to my mouth. "Are you hungry? I can order you something."

"Yes," I respond. "How long have I been in a coma?"

She smiles. "No coma," she says. "I will let the doctor know you are awake."

Before I can assess my situation, the doctor enters the room and looks me over. She clears her throat. I start to ask her a question when she stops me.

"Just listen. I will explain everything and answer all your questions."

I take another drink of water. "Before you begin," I listen to my own voice. "What kind of disaster was I in? I mean, how did I end up covered in blood so many times? I can't remember...."

"There was no disaster, per se, but I can explain everything, if you will just listen."

She opens her arms wide and smiles as if she has seen a vision of the Virgin Mary and she is mesmerized.

"Sometimes, although it hasn't happened for years now..." She pauses and then starts again. "Sometimes, during this procedure, when the nanites mix with someone's DNA, they enter the body and rewrite or remake certain organs. For example, if a heart valve needs to be repaired, or the patient has other defects, the nanites, reading the DNA of that individual, will recreate a more perfect specimen and correct the defect."

I wait, my brows furrowed.

She clears her throat. "In some cases, they get a bit over zealous and recreate an entire being. This is your situation."

She steps away from the bed.

"This is what you are saying happened to me? That I'm not me anymore?" I ask. "I am no longer myself? But, I can remember my life, my name—I have memories."

I start to panic and pull myself into a sitting position.

"Calm down!" Dr. Rushing urges.

The doctor glances at the nurse and she moves toward the bed with a hypodermic needle.

"No!" I shout. "Don't put me out again."

Dr. Rushing waves her away.

Before they can stop me, I jump up and put the bed between us. I feel cold, my legs are shaking, and I look down at my naked body, or at someone's naked body. For what I see is a slender young body with perky breasts, beautiful pale pink nipples, thin legs, and a flat stomach.

As I turn back to Dr. Rushing, her eyes beg me to reconsider the scream that is on my lips.

I swallow hard and move cautiously to the full-length mirror across the room. Wasn't it just a few days ago that I did this assessment of my body? It's like I stepped out of my old fat suit and put on a youthful one instead. It's me, but the lips are plumper, the skin is flawless, the eyelashes are fuller, longer, and the brows arch perfectly over bigger, brighter eyes of the truest blue. Her hair is like flowing silk, gently curling and rippling softly over youthful hands. The shine is like nothing I have ever seen in human hair and reminds me of the Dynel wigs that were popular in the 60s and 70s.

Her teeth are a bit smaller than mine. Her nose is shorter. All the things I would change if I could are better. Pushing hair out of the way, I peek at her ears. Little ears. At least that hasn't changed. I notice the nails have dried blood under them.

"Who is she?" I ask.

She tries to remain serious, but I hear the excitement in her voice. "She is you...a better you. She is your "do-over."

I tear my gaze from the new me and look up at Dr. Rushing's reflection in the mirror behind me. "How long has this transformation taken?"

"That's a problem. We contacted your family when we realized the project had started down this path."

She saw the anger in my eyes.

"It's been months," she admits. "Your husband has been here, demanding to see you. We let him see you while you were sleeping. He knows you will look different; younger. We tried to explain as much as we could."

"How many months?" I ask, watching my mouth move as I talk.

"Two months," Dr. Rushing replies.

I glance out the French Doors to the balcony and see a soft dusting of snow. "Two months?" A tear falls from my eye. It had been late summer when I arrived. "My granddaughter has probably forgotten me by now." How can it have been two months?

I was only aware of a small bit of it. "And I've been unconscious all that time?"

"It was better for you, to keep you sedated," she explains. "You were experiencing a lot of pain."

I stare at myself in the mirror, while Dr. Rushing goes

through the full scope of my transformation, down to the cellular level, speaking with words I cannot understand. I continue to turn; first this way, then backwards looking over my shoulder.

"Now what," I ask. "How old am I?"

"Chronologically twenty-three, no more than twenty-five."

"I want to go home." I turn to face Dr. Rushing directly.

"We suggest staying here at the clinic for some time to see if there will be any more changes."

"You mean I could still change?" I ask.

"We don't know. Like I said, this hasn't happened for ten years."

"There are others like me?" I ask. "Will I suddenly age?"

"We don't know. Everyone is different. Although we have never had anyone suddenly age. We would like you to go through a psychological test." She gave a brief smile. "You know, talk to a psychologist to see how this will affect you. To prepare you…"

"Prepare me for what?" I ask.

"Some families have difficulties with such changes."

"My family loves me!" I say in defiance.

"Yes," says Dr. Rushing, "the old you. How they will accept the new you or the new package is difficult to say."

I shiver and hug myself.

The nurse reaches into the closet and pulls out my robe. The belt now wraps around my waist twice. I scowl as I try to free my hair from my robe. "Cut this, will you?" I ask the nurse. "Do you have any scissors?"

"No!" counters Dr. Rushing. "You can't do anything like that right now. Besides," she says defeated, "in our experience, it will only grow back in a few days."

"What?" I ask.

She sighs. "That's the other part we need to discuss."

She invites me to sit at the table. "Please, Opal."

I move to the table and sit down, picking up the spoon in front of me to taste the steaming soup before me. "Ouch! Hot!"

"New tissues in your mouth. Like a child, it will take some time to get used to things," she explains. "You will have to build up muscles, develop a tolerance to sunlight, cold, and wearing clothes."

A tear falls from my eye. It feels hot.

"The nanites keep you in a state of perfection. If you get a cut, they repair it. If you cut off your finger, another one will eventually grow in its place. They will repair organs, fight free radicals and inflammation."

"Can I age?" I ask.

"Not really."

"Am I immortal?"

"Not really, although we call those who have gone through the transformation imMEMortals."

"How long will I live?"

"We don't know. The first HuMEMs are still alive. They changed sixty years ago and still look youthful. There will come a time that you will be able to cut your hair, but not now. Not when you are so young...or newborn."

"Can't you just take the nanites out?" I ask.

"No. They are connected to you and reside in your organs." She sighs deeply. "It's complicated."

"Take them out with an MRI; it's magnetic." I suggest.

"They aren't metal so, that doesn't work." She chuckles. "Look," she says, "don't you think we have tried everything? They are like symbiotic bacteria that live in your systems helping you digest food, or fight infections. They need you to continue to exist. They survive on the electrical impulses in your body."

"So electrocute them!"

"It doesn't work." She shakes her head. "We have tried everything, believe me. Besides, being imMEMortal isn't so bad."

"ImMEMortal?" I try the name.

"Except you outlive everyone you love." I say. "What does it mean imMEMortal?"

"An M.E.M. is a micro-electronic machine or nanite.

They are microscopic machines that are programed to do one particular assignment."

I start to cry. "I just came here for my skin."

"And your skin is beautiful. The best I've ever seen."

"I can't be the only one!" I continue crying and shouting. "What about that young woman who was in the surgery with me. What happened to her?"

Her brow wrinkles.

"I saw her covered in blood."

"That was you, Opal. You must have seen your reflection in the metal cabinets." She looks startled.

I start putting the images together. No wonder she looked familiar.

"Does anyone ever die?"

"Yes, there have been casualties." Her voice becomes quiet. "The nanites usually divide up and work simultaneously on different organs. However, there have been times that a person was in need of such great repair that they all concentrated on one organ to the detriment of the entire body." She sighs. "Only a few. There are also patients with compromised DNA and the transMEM didn't turn out so well for them."

"How many people are there like me?"

"Fifty or so."

"Really?" I am stunned.

"Yes, really, including the young couple that picked you up at the airport," she says.

I think back to them and shake my head. "Yeah, they are different. Zoe and Lonnie have a certain look about them, like life glows inside their skin."

"Exactly!" Dr. Rushing smiles. "And now, you have that glow. How do you feel?"

"My joints feel liquidy. Unstuck." I move my legs and test my knees. "Really unstuck!" I admit. "No pain or creaks. My neck feels loose and I can see everything." I licked my lips. "My mouth feels a bit tender."

"Yeah," she says as she writes something on a notepad, "That was the last thing that changed. You just grew these new teeth. Smile," she says, sticking her finger in my mouth and pulling my lips aside. "Just give it a week or so and you'll be fine."

She rose to leave. "Remember, Heike has your schedule for tomorrow. We need to build you up first by exercising those new muscles, then you will need to visit the doctors for a complete physical and stress test, and visit the psychologist for evaluation. You also need to get used to being in your own body."

"Clothes?" I question.

"We'll have some delivered. Shoes, under things. Use a new toothbrush and no makeup. Let's give everything a chance to settle."

Makeup? I am breathtakingly beautiful. Why would I use makeup? My reflection draws me back to the mirror.

"Can I make a call to my husband?"

"Sure, but wait until after…"

"I see the psychologist." I finish.

She smiles and leaves the room.

I look at the nurse. "Now what?"

"How about a bath?" she says.

I look at my grimy nails. "Good idea."

CHAPTER 4

I stay in my room the rest of the day. Sometimes, I sit in the Wintergarten; sometimes, I just sit in front of the TV. So much has happened in the world in two months; earthquakes, floods, wars, and divorces in Hollywood.

I glance at my image in the mirror. I keep moving the mirror so I can look at myself wherever I sit. This person is a complete stranger. Most of the time, I see my old self before the new one comes into focus. I am rather embarrassed by the new me. She is sexy without trying. Very coquettish and flirty...to me. I don't know if she is trying to get me to like her, or begging for acceptance. But then I remind myself that she is me.

I finally get into bed, but not without first peeking into the mirror for a final appraisal. I am wearing my pajamas I brought with me. The bottoms have an elasticized waist, but still fall to the floor if I release them. The top swallows me and I look like a little girl wearing her mother's clothes.

I am cold and I don't think I will ever get warm. The nurse comes in to see if I need anything. She is kind and brings me a heated blanket. I eventually fall asleep.

New clothes finally appear in the morning, so I slip into the sports bra and tiny panties. I find myself laughing out loud as I pull them on. They are small enough for a little girl, but stretch to fit my new little bottom. In my new yoga pants, t-shirt, sweater, socks, and running shoes I look even younger and thinner.

I feel exhausted just getting dressed. How long will it take me to get up and moving? For several weeks, I do slow paced exercise. I have to practice walking, turning, reaching with my arms, and touching my toes. I work out hours every day, until I can maneuver on my own. Then Dr. Rushing says I am ready for the battery of tests they have prepared for me.

I pass the stress tests and ace the physicals. I get another big laugh, when Dr. Rushing tells me I am a virgin. So much for the hysterectomy, I have a new womb. Monthly visits from Mother Nature will begin soon.

She says there is no evidence that I have had surgery. The scar from my shoulder surgery is gone; there are no varicose veins in my legs, no fillings, caps, or crowns in my teeth. Everything is new again. I can hear everything, see anything, and have great physical endurance.

After lunch, I go to meet with the psychologist. This I am not looking forward to, because as much as I have changed in appearance, I still have problems on the inside. I know I have some major character flaws, dealing with guilt and accepting that everything isn't my fault. I'm a mess!

What is that saying? *"If only you could be young again, but still retain all the knowledge life has given."*

Well, this is my do over. Having all life's experiences doesn't just give you an edge, it also comes with limitations and doubts about who you are and what you can accomplish. Changing the outward appearance hasn't changed the emotional cripple inside.

I meet with the psychologist every day. She helps me understand that the way other people behave is not a result of my actions. I have always blamed myself for the bad behavior of others.

If Preston yells and screams about something, I feel it's always my fault and that if I'd done something different he wouldn't treat me like he does. Slowly, I come to understand that the way others respond to situations is their problem, not mine. I am only accountable for my own actions.

My father had a bad temper when I was young and I felt it was my burden to hide his bad behavior from others. He always said, "Now look what you've made me do." So I took on the responsibility to hide his anger, or make it seem that I was guilty of making him angry.

I always thought that someday I could make him see his bad attitude and poor behavior. I thought that if I worked really hard, taking on more chores or smiling more, it would change who he was.

The psychologist also helps me understand that everyone has a choice in how they respond to outside stimulus. It isn't up to anybody else to cover up another's bad behavior. Perhaps if I hadn't, other people would have seen who he was and his own embarrassment would have helped him change.

Two weeks have passed and I haven't changed physically. The doctors feel that I have reached the end of my "growth period", but I have a strange feeling that something different is taking place inside of me. Maybe it is the talks with the psychologist. I could have sworn I was being followed yesterday. Maybe paranoia is part of the "growth" package.

Zoe is taking me to town to do some shopping. I have been wearing the same hand-me-downs and single pair underwear for too long. I wash the one pair of undies I have, but after a workout or a run, I don't want to put them back on after I've showered.

I'm so excited. I haven't been to a real city since I arrived at the clinic ten weeks ago and I'm long overdue for a break from the constant tests and examinations. Zoe says she is taking me to St. Gallen, the biggest town to our mountain. A few days ago, I had a short trip with Zoe to Teufen, a lovely Swiss village, but I stayed in the car while Zoe ran in to get the mail. I wanted to get out and explore, but she said it should wait for another time.

We take the Land Rover down the mountain to the crowded town and Zoe parks so we can take the tram to the shopping area. I have a blast shopping in the "junior" department, buying jeans and sweaters, boots, socks, bras and panties, PJs, and silk underclothes (aka fancy Long Johns) to keep me warm. I buy a doll for my sweet granddaughter Lucy and chocolate for her mother, as requested.

We pile all the packages in the car and start looking for a place to dine. Once again, I feel like I'm being watched and turn around to see two guys following us. I warn Zoe and she says we will duck into the next shop and see if they follow. By the time we reach the shop, another fellow has joined them. We dash through the door of the next store and lose ourselves in an array of knitwear. They don't follow us into the shop, so I decide that I'm just being paranoid.

When we finally reach the restaurant, we ask to be seated at a table by the window. As we chat, I watch the people milling about with their umbrellas; it is raining in the lower elevations. Then I noticed Zoe staring at me.

"What's wrong?" I ask.

"You are positively glowing; an unnatural glow," she whispers. "And you stink!"

Then we realize all conversation in the place has stopped and every man in the restaurant is looking at me.

Several come over to our table and start arguing amongst themselves, pushing one another.

One man starts showing me his strength by lifting Zoe in her chair, and smiling at me. Another asks me what perfume I am wearing and leans on the table with his elbows, holding his head in his hands and asking if I would dance with him. *I don't hear any music.* Another sits at my feet and lays his head against my leg, looking up at me like he is high on something. The waiter sets an entire tray of desserts on our table, asking if he can offer some sweets for the sweet.

Their wives and girlfriends are calling to them, trying to get their attention. Pure pandemonium breaks out; the men are shouting at one another and their women are begging them to stop their bizarre behavior.

Zoe hops out of her seat, grabs my arm and marches me towards the exit. "I don't know what is going on with you, but we need to get you out of here."

I abscond with a few pastries as Zoe herds me out the door. She pushes me onto the first tram and before we arrive at the car park, several men on the bus are already trying to get near me.

"So," I say, "I'm not being paranoid, they really are following me!" We keep moving towards the door.

"What's happening to me?" I ask.

"I don't know," she says.

Looking over at me, she ponders, "Maybe it is some kind of pheromone overdose the nanites are giving you. It is your first menses and your first time being exposed to so many men. Maybe they are trying to make you attractive to a mate."

"Did this happen to you?" I ask her.

"No."

We jump off the bus and dash to the car, making it out of town and up the mountain without anyone else following us. Zoe phones Dr. Rushing and rattles on about what happened.

What does this mean? It hadn't happened to Zoe, so why me? Tears run down my face as the whole experience overwhelms me. I just want to go home and be normal. I don't want to be a freak with glowing skin and mate-attracting musk!

I miss my family, especially my precious Lucy. I consider how this whole mess will affect my relationship with her, my sweet daughter, and overbearing husband. I want to be near Lucy as much as possible, to have a relationship with her that will last the rest of my normal existence of twenty years or more.

I think of all the dreams I have for what Lucy and I will share: shopping trips and lunches together; trips to museums, the opera, the symphony; travel to Paris and Rome. I want to see her go to the prom and get married — now I don't know if I'll be able to do any of that.

Zoe's voice brings me back to the present. "She's upset!" she tells the doctor before hanging up her phone.

"I'll be alright," I say, wiping the tears from my cheeks. "At least, I think I will, if these damn nanites don't kill me first."

I feign a smile.

"That's a girl!" She says, patting my leg. "Keep a stiff upper lip! We'll figure out what is going on with them."

"How old are you?" I ask.

"About twenty-seven," she says. "Still."

"No," I counter, "really; in real years?"

"I was about twenty-five when I had the procedure." She glances my way. "That was about sixty years ago." Zoe coughs nervously. "I don't like to talk about myself."

"Why?" I ask.

"Because, my reasons for the procedure weren't the same as everybody else's. I had a deformity that made me choose to change my appearance at a young age. Dr. Rushing's mentor, Dr. Heinrick Englesteine, preformed my transMEM."

She shudders. "Remembering is a bitch!"

I won't press her for her story.

"Wow," I chuckle. "You're an old woman, eighty-five!"

She smiles, shaking her head. "Wisdom and beauty are

a heady combination! There's Teufen!" She indicates the village as we pass by.

"I would love to explore it someday," I say, staring out the window. It appears to be an idyllic Swiss Village, covered in a fine layer of newly fallen snow, twinkling in the evening air. The chalets, with their low hanging roofs are dusted with snow, while the flower boxes, on the balcony rails, still yield red and blue blooms.

I sigh. "Just beautiful."

"In my experience, beauty is often a cover for something deadly." Zoe says.

I think of my own beauty covering a festering tangle of emotions which still possesses me, and probably will until the day I die. Huh! If I die? I am anxious to hear Zoe's story, but I know she isn't ready to tell me. Deformed? Wonder what that could mean?

Actually, this procedure would be great for those who had to look at life through a debilitating deformity. It could bring sight to the sightless; sound to the deaf, birth to the barren, repair minds. I wonder if it can rebuild lives destroyed by disease, like MS, or Parkinson's?

This operation could offer hope to many suffering people, as long as it is in the control of those with good intentions. In the wrong hands, it could be used as a weapon to develop an army of eternal soldiers who can heal themselves, or to make someone very rich by selling the procedure for millions of dollars to the elite. What wouldn't someone give to have "eternal" life or the promise of life without disease?

I wonder how this clinic and Dr. Rushing have been able to keep all of this a secret. With so many people coming to the clinic, surely the secret of what happened to me, and others would get out.

What did Dr. Rushing say? It's been ten years since they've had a transformation like mine? Is it a blessing or curse? The jury is still out on that one. I shiver and rub my arms.

"Cold?" Zoe asks as she reaches to turn up the heater.

"No, just felt like someone walked across my grave."

When we arrive back at the Spa, it's dinner time and Dr. Rushing meets us at the door. We quickly return to my room. Another doctor who assisted with my transMEM, Dr. Mendahl, is waiting for us.

As we sit at the table and begin to eat dinner, Dr. Mendahl starts breathing heavily. He tells Dr. Rushing that he is finding me very attractive and excuses himself.

She smiles briefly. "Well, you are having an interesting day, aren't you?

"How long am I going to continue in this period of heat?" I ask.

"As far as I know," she laughs, "it hasn't happened before. Each transformation is different and whenever someone changes," she leans forward at the table, her hands running through her hair, "we never know what to expect. There is always something new we must deal with. This is just a hiccup. I have no doubt it will end soon."

Several men in scrubs bring in my packages, taking more than casual interest in me. One leaves the room and returns with a bouquet of flowers that I had seen setting on a table in the foyer. Dr. Rushing shakes her head at their antics and orders them out of the room.

"Obviously, we will need to isolate you from the male population at the Spa. Please, stay in your room until further notice. I will arrange for you to have exercise in the gardens." She shrugs her shoulders. "Hope you bought some boots and winter clothes."

I see nothing but women for the next week. They do the housekeeping around my room, take my vital signs and do my daily evaluations. I eat with women, walk with women, talk with women, and visit women.

I'm sweating constantly and everything I wear smells. I have to keep changing my t-shirts and my pits reek a musky odor. It isn't a bad scent, I am told, but is very overpowering.

Dr. Rushing says the men can smell me on the other side of the building. I mainly stay in the marble bath with lavender bath salts to mask my odor.

A few days later, the sweats subside and my body odor seems to have returned to normal. Once again, I can move about freely within the Spa. I throw out the "scented" T-shirts and Zoe buys new ones when she goes to town.

"No use keeping these around." She jokes that she will keep a couple and wear them when she is in the mood for a little lovemaking.

"Wish we could bottle that scent." Dr. Rushing is quite excited. "We've never had this happen before." She laughs. "You must have something rather primitive about your DNA that made the nanites do this."

"Do you think it will happen again?" I ask timidly.

She guffaws.

"Wouldn't that be something? You will have to lock yourself in every time it happens. Men will be drooling over you and fighting one another. Showing how they would be the perfect specimen for a mate."

She laughs until she cries.

"Oh, dear," she says, seeing my face. "I guess it isn't really funny! Poor you!"

My first morning back in the general population, I look around the dining room at breakfast, wondering how many other people are here for the skin procedure. Everyone seems to all be my age—my real age.

An older woman takes the chair next to me.

"What are you doing here young lady?" she asks. "Don't tell me you are having work on your pretty little body!"

I smile. "No, actually I've already had my procedure. Haven't they done a marvelous job on me? I used to be older than you!"

I pick up my tea tray and leave the dining room, grinning to myself. Let that sink in!

She stares after me. Probably thinks I'm rude. Guess I am!

That evening, I find a pair of scissors and impulsively cut ten inches off my hair. It grows back by the end of the week, but I think it might be a bit shorter. I ask Dr. Rushing why my hair stays this length. She says it is just the way the nanites interpret my genes and that I am lucky my hair doesn't drag the floor like Marta's.

CHAPTER 5

Who is Marta?

Over the next week, Zoe introduces me to many of the other HuMems. Every one of them is the best specimen their DNA can provide. They are beautiful. Some have lovely skin that glows, while others are mellower. One woman in particular doesn't glow at all.

One evening, while soaking in a hot bath, I begin to feel flushed. It is exactly like the hot flashes I used to get when I was going through menopause after my hysterectomy. I open my eyes and my entire body is aglow. My heartbeat increases dramatically and I start to panic. Then with a bright flash, the heat subsides. I wonder what this new phenomenon means. Maybe the water is too hot, or I've been in the water too long. Could they become water logged? Overheated?

I quickly grab my robe and phone Zoe. I explain what happened and ask her if she has experienced anything similar. Of course, she says no. I am a freak among freaks! Why can't I just be like the others?

The next day, Zoe introduces me to the lovely Marta. Her hair is double-braided, heavy, and thick as an arm, hanging below her knees. But it is her honey brown skin that fascinates me. It is so beautiful, like a suntan when it turns a golden brown, with just enough glow. She has large green eyes with yellow sparkles and a lovely smile, with small white teeth. Her stature is petite and very graceful. Her voice sounds musical—child-like. She is so beautiful; my eyes are teary. I realize I'm staring at her unabashedly when I finally grasp that Zoe is calling to me some moments later.

The next morning, I wake to find my appearance has changed. I don't know what to make of my reflection in the mirror. My skin has turned the same beautiful color as Marta's and my eyes are lavender. Dr. Rushing is enthralled with the changes and questions me about my responses when I met Marta. I tell her about my appreciation for Marta's skin color, and that I had thought how beautiful it would look with lavender eyes.

She has me think of something I would like to change about my appearance. I stared at myself in the mirror and say that I am pleased with the change.

She says, "It is an experiment, just pick something small."

I say I could use thick eyelashes and more defined brows.

Nothing happens, thank God. The last changes I went through were so painful and I have been through enough pain to last a lifetime. I don't want any more experimenting. I am happy with who I am.

Dr. Rushing says she wants to do some further tests in the morning. She says the MEMs inside me are more advanced than she has ever experienced.

Back in my room, I cut another ten inches off my hair that night. By the time I am ready for bed, my skin color is back to normal, as is my eye color. At least there was no pain; I didn't feel a thing. Maybe a little stinging in my eyes, but I just thought they felt a little dry.

The next morning, Dr. Rushing and her assistant are surprised to see that my skin color has reverted to its normal tone and my eyes have returned to a beautiful blue. I report no discomfort, other than the dry feeling in my eyes.

They are set up to do a sonogram. During the test, Dr. Rushing keeps saying things like "Oh, look here. Where does this one go?" and "Wow, can you believe that?" and "This is remarkable!"

Meanwhile, I'm standing naked, covered in gel as they run the wand up and down my body. I am shivering and my teeth are chattering when they finally notice me.

"Quick," says Dr. Rushing, "get her into a hot shower."

I am so glad to stand and let the steamy water run over me. After some time, I dress and quickly leave by another door. I can hear them in the office talking animatedly about their findings, but I want to escape and be alone for a while.

Back in my room, I dry my hair, put on a knitted hat and a wooly jumper to go for a walk in the gardens. The flowerbeds are snow covered, but the silence is amazing. This is a place where I can gather my thoughts and write in the journal the psychologist wants me to do as a sort of cathartic release.

MEMs! I know this is advanced technology, but having it inside of me is overwhelming. What the MEMs do affects me and my life. Maybe I should have been more grateful and satisfied with my life. I have a husband who loves me and child and grandchild who adore me. Maybe I wasn't as beautiful as a menopausal woman as I am now; I was a little overweight, with a few chin whiskers, some wrinkles and graying hair, but at least I was safe.

Now my future is unsure. Will my husband still want me? Am I to be thrust out of my home and left to fend for myself? Will my daughter and granddaughter still love me?

What percentage of a person's appearance determines how much they are loved? I never really felt unloved before, although I never felt worthy of someone's love. I thought it was my appearance that was keeping my husband from making love to me. Maybe it is my own feelings of inadequacy that makes me feel I don't deserve his love.

Zoe had said that being beautiful is about believing in

yourself and knowing that you only need to please yourself. Waiting for the approval of others is like wading through their shortcomings. Who wants to do that?

Now, I'm rather pretty, but what does that mean to me? My husband will either be excited to have the freedom to make love to a younger woman without feeling like he is cheating on his wife, or he will feel that I'm like a daughter and won't want anything to do with me. I mean, I don't have to look at me. I only have to live here in this gorgeous body. It is easy to forget I'm young again.

This is my "do over" Dr. Rushing said. I spend more time writing in my journal and thinking about my future. I have decided I want to go home and return to my life as much as I can. I will have to make some sacrifices, but it is better than being completely isolated from my loved ones.

I rise to leave and hear a loud whoosh, as an arrow pierces my right thigh. I scream in pain and suddenly people are rushing to my side to help.

"What the hell?" Charlie, the grounds keeper, lets Zoe and Heike help me to the clinic while he takes off running through the woods toward the only direction the arrow could have come.

"My God, who would try to kill me? I ask. "If I hadn't got up to leave, it would have hit me in the back!"

Dr. Rushing isn't at the clinic, but her assistant, Heike

takes me in the room where she administers a sedative. She waits a while to remove the arrow.

"The MEMs will make quick work on repairing the wound," she says.

I'm not in any pain, so the sedative must be working.

Charlie, the grounds keeper, wasn't able to find anyone, but he thinks it was probably a hunter that had wandered into the clinic's woods. They must have taken off when they heard me scream.

"There are NO TRESSPASSING signs, but it is hunting season," he says.

He pats my hand as he explains, "They aren't allowed to hunt in many towns, but they are allowed in the forests."

I pick up the arrow and examine it. "Wow," I say, turning it over in my hands. "Can they really kill deer with these old arrows?"

Charlie takes the arrow from me to examine it. "I don't know what happened to this arrow," he says. "But, it isn't age." He walks over to where Heike is looking through a microscope.

"I'm already on it, Charlie," she says. "Not a known acid. The MEMs have made quick work of breaking it down."

"How can they do that?" I ask. "Aren't they just polymers and organic matter?"

"Acids are organic," she says, pulling off a pair of

rubber gloves. She is in deep thought and pulls at them nervously, making them snap.

Heike pulls her cell phone out of her white jacket pocket to call Dr. Rushing. She talks hurriedly, telling Dr. Rushing about the shooting and the arrow.

"I know it is the MEMs, because one was left behind and I have it isolated on a slide." What?" She counters. "I'll see." She walks back to the microscope. "You're right," she speaks again. "It is different than it was; a little larger, but different in appearance. "Wait, it is doing something." She lays down the phone, but keeps talking on speakerphone. "I think it is trying to use some kind of acid on the slide."

Dr. Rushing's voice echoes around us from the speaker. "Put it in the neutralizer…just the nanite. Then examine the slide to see what kind of solution it is using. It can only use what is available to it in the host's body."

Host? My brain works the word over in my mind. Host? My body isn't mine anymore? I am the host? They are what? Parasites? Parasites that control me? I mumble to no one. I feel sick. Good thing I am sitting on the examination table or I would drop to the floor.

"There's an echo," Dr. Rushing shouts. "I'm on my way back up the mountain." Then silence.

"Heike turns and looks at me. "Now look," she starts, "they aren't really parasites. They aren't in control. They follow your directions."

"Oh yeah," I say. "I wanted them to turn me into Marta and I wanted them to make me desirable to men and find me a mate! Imagine what they will do to any child I might have!"

I am shouting and crying at the same time. I am angry and horrified. "I just want to go back to being me. I want to go home!"

Heike and Charlie stare at one another.

"Do you want me to give you something?" She asks, turning to me.

"You mean to calm me down?" I shout. "Yeah, give me a pill, a shot, a shrink! That should take care of the problem! What I need is for you and the good doctor to remove these damn things! You can cook up a problem, but you can't fix one you've made!"

I start to gasp for air. "Now what?" I rasp, grasping my neck. "They are killing me!"

The room begins to spin and the light dims...

Later, I wake up in my room and there's no light shining through my French doors. I rub my eyes and take a quick check in the bathroom mirror. Everything seems normal.

A voice speaks. "You hungry?" It's Dr. Rushing. She was sleeping on the sofa.

"Yeah," I said. "What happened?" I return to the

bedroom.

"You passed out. I'm sorry this is happening to you, Opal. Sit." She pats the empty seat next to her on the couch and continues in a quiet voice.

"While you were out, we were able to do a CAT scan. The MEMs have made a kind of chain mail layer over your heart. They used the metal from the arrowhead. They are trying to protect you...to protect themselves. We've never seen anything like this; it's unprecedented. You are the first HuMEM in which the nanites appear to have come close to being sentient. They are evolving. Thinking. Making decisions by themselves."

"I'm becoming a monster." I whisper. "You have to do something! Heaven knows I'm not in control. They do whatever they want!"

"I believe you will soon have communication with them."

"If they can read my thoughts, they have access to my brain. Then I'll have no control."

Tears flood down my face and drip off my chin.

"Why did they choke me earlier?"

"While you were out?" she asks. "I didn't want to tell you, but you need to know."

She puts on a serious expression, but I can tell she is trying not to smirk. "You were angry and they readied you for battle."

"Huh?"

"They covered your facial skin with barbs. They weren't metal, just keratin...hard organic material. They looked like sharp thorns."

She handed me her iPad with a picture she had taken of my barbed face.

"Great! I'm ready for the Freak Show at the circus!" I exclaim, horrified. "Please, Dr. Rushing, take them out; I want to go home." I whimpered.

She shakes her head. "You can't. Not yet. Not until we know the extent of your possession."

"My possession? You said they are multiplying?"

"Yes. There are many more than I injected. They seem to be able to replicate themselves."

"Will they keep multiplying?"

"Hey," she turns to face me. "If the government gets wind of this, they will come and take you. Then no one will ever see you again. I really am trying to help you. Let me do that will you?"

She grasps my hands. "If nothing new develops in the next few months, you can make a trip to meet your husband and talk about things."

"A visit?"

"A visit. You'll gain a better perspective of what

emotions your family will go through by gauging how your husband responds to the new you. It hasn't worked out for anyone who has tried it and they always return to Switzerland where they are in touch with others like themselves. We have a community of HuMEMs here.

I vow then and there to try to communicate with the nanites and make them understand we are prisoners if they don't lie low. No more evolving!

A few days later, I take a trip to town to make a few purchases. There are no unexpected events and it feels liberating to just get away by myself. I buy some more souvenirs for my family and return to the mountain in time for dinner.

CHAPTER 6

That evening, I put my plan to try communicating with the nanites into action. I step into the warm marble bath and watch the candlelight flicker on the tile. The flow begins just as I start to feel comfortable. My head tingles and I am amazed as I watch my reflection in the tile. My head glows blue as small energy ribbons ripple through my skin, like I'm some kind of exhibit at the Science Museum back home.

I wait silently while the MEMs work to create mental pathways. I try communicating with them by concentrating on one word: cold.

Nothing happens. I wait and think that perhaps this is a hopeless cause. Then, just as I'm ready to give up, my skin pinks like I am blushing and I instantly warm up. It is a small thing, but it worked! Just to make sure it wasn't a fluke, I try again; this time, with something more involved; webbed toes. I concentrate hard, imagining a picture of webbed feet that I had seen in a medical journal once.

Finally, my toes begin to tingle and burn. When I lift one foot out of the water, there's a membrane of skin between my toes! It's so fine; my fingers tear it as I pull my toes apart to examine them. I smile. What else can I train them to understand with my feelings and thoughts?

Suddenly, someone is banging on my bathroom door.

"Opal!" Zoe yells my name. Then I hear her trying to open the locked door.

I take a moment to calm myself, tell the MEMs to disappear, and my head goes back to normal. I wrap my head with a towel and quickly grab my robe before I open the door.

"What's the matter?"

Zoe looks at me quizzically. "What was all that bright flashing light I saw coming from under the door?"

Dr. Rushing barged into the bathroom before I could answer. She is breathing like she ran laps.

"Oh, just a lamp I picked up for my granddaughter." I pointed to a lamp sitting on the bench. The shade is slowly spinning and the light projects shapes of animals overhead.

"No," she says, pushing me aside. "It was a really bright flashing light; like a strobe."

"It must have been when the candles were lit and I had the lamp on its side, examining the bottom. Also, I took out this light." I held it up. "I think it is like a strobe light. I replaced it with this bulb with a warmer glow."

"A strobe?" Zoe examined the bulb in my hand. She looks up with anger and yanks off the towel covering my hair.

"Your hair isn't wet." She says.

"I know," I answer. "I put the towel on to keep it from getting wet while I was bathing."

Zoe sighs heavily and walks across the room. "Why didn't you tell anyone you were going to town?"

"What is this? Am I a prisoner here? I don't answer to you! I believe I am old enough to go to town without a chaperone."

Dr. Rushing shushes us. "Come on girls. Zoe, she isn't your responsibility. However, Opal, you should have let someone know what you were going to do and where you were going."

"I did." I interject to stop the lecture. "I left a message on Zoe's voicemail, and I also left a message on your machine at the lab, where you told me you were going to be. Besides, Lonnie gave me the keys to the Land Rover, so he knew."

"Now," I move them out of the bathroom and into the hall outside my bedroom door. "I would like to get dressed, go to sleep, and get an early start in the morning."

"What's happening in the morning?" Zoe asks.

"I'm making arrangements to meet my husband in Guatemala. He has some work to do there and we thought that would be the best place to meet and talk."

I smile sweetly. But, before I can shut the door, Dr. Rushing smiles and points to the lamp in my hand. "That won't work in the US; different voltage."

"Hmmm." I say shutting the bedroom door and locking it.

"We can talk in the morning." I hear Dr. Rushing talking to Zoe as they retreat down the hallway. "Everything will be alright."

"You know she can't go home!" Zoe whispers loudly.

I sigh and look at myself in the mirror. There isn't any evidence of MEM activity.

After a restless night, I wake with a start. My arms feel strange and when I examine them, they are covered in feathers! My dream encroaches on my thoughts.

I dreamt I was a beautiful white bird in flight, hovering over my house back in Nashville and flying over Laura's home. Lucy and I played together until her mother came out to see whom she was talking. "Oh Mother!" she said, recognizing me. "You are such a beautiful bird! But you aren't family." Then she started chasing me with a broom.

I brush my hand along my arm and the feathers disperse like ash. They aren't real feathers and although there are a few in my hair, they seem to be mainly located on my arms. On closer examination, I can see that they are made of dried skin that dissolves with the slightest touch.

This is a problem. It is evident the nanites have access to my thoughts, whether conscious or unconscious, but they aren't able tell the difference between a dream and reality. I could be in big trouble, which means I can't leave the Spa until I gain control of them.

I think about this the entire next day. How can they know my dreams? I need to talk with Dr. Rushing, without revealing what is happening to me.

I feel like I am being watched and there are things I'm not being told. How else would they have known something was going on in my room when I was communicating with the MEMs? I've even checked my room for bugs and hidden cameras—but find nothing.

The next morning, I wake up with huge breasts. They are so heavy, that I have to support them with my hands and make a sling with an oversized t-shirt. I escape into the bathroom and try to communicate with the nanites to make them go away. I feel unusually tired, so I find excuses to stay in my room. I'm reading; I'm depressed and want to be alone—It takes a couple of days for my giant breasts to return to their original size. Eventually, they return to a "normal" size, but are still noticeably bigger than they were before.

I'm going to have to buy new bras.

As soon as I sit down to breakfast the next morning, I am joined by Dr. Rushing.

"So, are you better today?" She asks. "Zoe and I were away for a few days, but I hear you were feeling depressed. I'm sorry you've been away from your family for so long, but it really is for the best."

"Yes, I'm better. All of this is just too much for me." I shook my head. "I'm alone. I need my family. I need some sort of a normal life. I want to go home and be regular old me."

Dr. Rushing blows out her breath like she has been holding it. "It's been quite a journey for you." She says quietly, looking into her cup. "I guess when I put myself in your shoes; I can understand how you must feel. We've been through it before with others." She stares into my eyes. "Believe it or not, it's been much worse for them, than it has been for you."

She glances around the room. "Better we speak in the lab." She says, taking my arm and ushering me down the hall. I jump up on the examination table while she paces.

"Not to change the subject, but I do have something I want to ask you." I take a deep breath. "How would the nanites know the difference between my actual experiences and dreams? Are they programmed? Are they little computers with lots of stored memory? Are they able to store information?"

"Yes, they are given some information. They each have different abilities and knowledge about how a human body functions; but only in elementary terms. They are prepared to follow DNA and construct protein from stored sources of amino acids that enables them to quickly create cells. Your

DNA is like a blueprint to creating a perfect specimen of you. Somehow, these MEMs have pooled their information and made it available to the collective."

Her eyes light up. "The nanites in you have built a network of neural pathways to your brain that surpasses anything we have ever seen. They are sentient, multiplying, evolving on their own. They read your thoughts; they are learning."

"What about dreams or unconscious thoughts? Can they act on them?"

"Zoe found a white feather in the hallway outside your door. It was not a real feather and disintegrated like ash when she touched it. Was it a result of dreams?" she asks.

"Yes." I confess. "I dreamt I was a white bird and woke up covered in feathers!"

She nodded. "They are trying to interpret your dreams, but they wouldn't have any information about feathers so they made up a likeness—not the real thing."

She glanced at my breasts. "I see your bust size has increased," she says. "Is that why you stayed in your room? Did something worse happen?"

I nod. "They were huge two days ago." I confess. "I had trouble carrying them."

"Another dream?"

"Yes. I'm scared, Dr. Rushing. What if I dream

something really horrible? Could they make me do things I don't want?"

"I think you can communicate with them. Explain to them about dreams and conscious verses unconscious thoughts. They should know that they happen in different areas of the brain. Daydreams and desires in one area, while commands come from another."

"Maybe this will help you understand," she explains. "The part of the brain that control dreams is our limbic system, which is the most primitive part of the brain. It also controls emotions and directs instincts, sexual behavior, sex-drives, and the fight or flight responses. I think we can assume they have been creating pathways in this part of the brain. This is also where memories can be accessed, as well as the dopamine pathways, they are neurotransmitters involved in mood and increases in pleasure. So let's say they can access both your dreams and your memories.

"Can they understand when I speak directly to them? I have been working on that, sort of." I offer. "I gave simple commands and they complied."

"Like, what kind of commands?" she asks.

"I asked them to make my toes webbed and they did. Mind you, it wasn't anything great. The skin split apart when I touched them."

"That all?" She waits, writing on her pad.

"Um..." I hesitate. I don't want to share all my secrets, but this is getting serious. The nanites are acting on unconscious thoughts and dreams. Who knows where this will lead? I need any help she can give.

"I told them I was cold once and they made me warm up. My face got red and I goose bumped all over." I cringe remembering. "It almost hurt. It was a very strange sensation."

"Ouch," I say, wincing and pulling off my shoes and socks. "I think they've performed for you."

"They understood you, Opal!" she says. "You are definitely in communication with them." Dr. Rushing gushes over my feet for what seems like hours, taking pictures and talking incessantly about the webs between my toes.

"It was a memory of what they did." I explain, agitated. "When I was telling you, I could see in here ..." I pointed to my head. "They accessed my memories."

"I don't think they can access them on their own," she says. "I think you have to be actively thinking about something before they will act on it."

"I have time this morning. Let's have a look at their activity." Dr. Rushing performs a complete physical on me. "Your legs and butt look really thin and I can see your ribs."

"Well," I say, "they had to get the fat from some place to make bigger boobs."

Her assistant enters the room with the ultrasound

machine. She and Dr. Rushing goop me with gel and run the wand over my entire body. The conclusion is definitive. The nanites are hard at work with their neural connections. In addition, they are busy making a second heart.

Dr. Rushing tells me that I should warn them about making too many redundancies. Then, she wants to know why I have chain pie weights in my stomach along with a few nuts and bolts.

I have no idea why I have a stomach full of metal, and tell her so. I did have a picture of such things enter my mind's eye once or twice over the past couple of days. Am I sleep walking and taking advice from these parasites? I ask to be locked in my room at night. I don't want to roam the halls, doing who knows what when I'm asleep.

I realize that I need to spend more time trying to communicate with them. The first thing I do is imagine the bedroom door being locked at night and getting into bed.

I borrow a couple of books from Dr. Rushing about the brain and spend time studying maps of the brain. I try letting them know that when I am sleeping, my dreams and unconscious thoughts are not real. When I want them to do something, my thoughts will be located in a different area of the brain. I repeat this several times a day, until I decide that it is time to experiment and see what they've learned

Dr. Rushing orders a series of low radiation x-rays and

lets me know that the nanites have used the metal I had ingested. I also now have an additional spleen and gallbladder—Dr. Rushing tells me I really have to communicate with the nanites about redundancies. An extra heart is one thing, but this is getting ridiculous. They've even created additional villi in the small intestine for supplying the body with extra nutrients and amino acids.

It amazes me how quickly they work. They created an acid that broke down the arrowhead in just an hour, and now, in just a few days, they have dissolved the other metals I've ingested.

I keep getting mental images of things like spinach, broccoli, and certain fruits. I finally realize they are communicating with me about what they want me to eat. When I eat what they suggest, I can sense they are pleased.

I've been working on communication with them every day and there have been no more incidents of things I dream about showing up in real life. Soon, I'm allowed to take small trips by myself. I've been to Lichtenstein and Germany for brief trips where I went to museums and shopped for clothes and shoes. My favorite trip, I took with Zoe to Italy. We stayed for a week in Rome and I spent hours just walking around looking at the sights. I loved the Vatican Museum and spent two days getting through it.

Zoe told me some of her story and we grew very close.

She was glad for the chance to let her hair down and forget all the staunch rules she lived by at the Clinic. We laughed, shouted, and went to several clubs, staying out until 4 a.m., dancing and enjoying our "youth."

We ride the trains when we travel and I love falling asleep to the sound of the clickety-clack of the tracks.

When we return, I spend time with Zoe and her husband, Lonnie, at their place at Lake Constance. It's so picturesque here; I love the quiet beauty and the secure feeling of being surrounded by hills and mountains. I sketch and read while Zoe and Lonnie go off by themselves. I don't mind being alone in such beautiful surroundings—it gives me time to ponder my situation and plan a course of action

When we return to the clinic, I decide it's time to tell Dr. Rushing that I've ordered the nanites to leave my body and they have. I give her a napkin that has about three dozen nanites in it.

She asks how I managed to get them to leave, and I explain that I pictured a scene from the movie *The Fantastic Voyage*, where the scientists exited the body through the tear ducts. I said I didn't know if that was all of them and she said she thought that there couldn't be many more than that.

I tell her that I hope they're all gone and that this episode is over. I know it really isn't, but I feel like this is the only way I'll be allowed to go home and return to my life.

What Dr. Rushing doesn't know is that I snuck into the lab the night we returned from Lake Constance, found a vial of nanites, and passed them off as mine. I did actually try to get them to leave, as I had told her, but they refused.

I expect every day for Dr. Rushing to tell me they saw me on video sneaking into the lab, but I never hear a word about the theft.

Now that they have no reason to keep me at the clinic, Preston and I arrange for our meeting in Guatemala. He says he is anxious to speak with me about something. I am a bit reluctant to have this conversation. Somehow, I just know that whatever it is Preston wants, it won't benefit me.

As the day approaches for me to leave, Dr. Rushing declares me nanite-free and gives her blessing for me to depart. She isn't very encouraging, though, telling me that I will be back soon enough.

She warns me repeatedly that this technology needs to be kept private and out of government hands. She is certain that if the wrong people find out about me, they will appropriate her research, which includes me, for their own agenda. I promise to keep my secret and tell no one.

CHAPTER 7

Preston meets me at the airport in Guatemala City, but he doesn't recognize me. I just stand there, watching him for a while. His hair is longer than he usually wears it and he has that vacation look; well rested and tanned. He's dressed casually and my heart flips as I realize I am still attracted to him and excited to see him. He is scowling and looks impatient, so I step forward and take his arm.

"Preston," I raise my voice to be heard above the excited Spanish clamor. He turns to me, but jerks his arm away, clearly startled at being touched by a stranger.

He seems not to recognize me. "Yes, I'm Preston Sanders." His eyes narrow. "Who are you?"

"Now, who do you think I am?" I say.

"Opal?" His eyebrows arch in shock.

"Yes, it's me."

He steps back and rakes his eyes over me, from head to toe. "You're a....a child." He pushes me further away holding me by the shoulders. "Is this a joke? Is someone trying to be funny?" He looks annoyed, almost angry.

I sigh, disappointed with his reaction. "It's me." I say. "They said you came to see me when I was changing."

"Yeah," he says, "but you were in bandages and I couldn't stay long. You were in very bad shape."

The look on his face tells me he's more than unhappy, maybe even appalled by my appearance.

"I don't think this is a good idea. You aren't you anymore. It's not good for me to be seen with such a young wife." He hisses under his breath.

He is embarrassed by me and I'm crushed by this knowledge. After all I've been through and as beautiful as I have become, it's still not enough. His rejection stabs my heart.

"Please," I whisper. "Let's just talk. No one knows us here, so nobody knows I'm your wife."

"I have several meetings and a golf date." His demeanor grows cold as he proceeds to lay out his itinerary.

"Surely you have time to talk with me about what we should do. You said you needed to see me and talk about things that have changed in our lives, and now you're telling me you have to play golf!"

"Okay, we'll talk." He sighs, resigned and clearly wanting to avoid a scene. He takes my arm and leads me or rather, drags me to the luggage carousel.

Outside the airport, we catch a small bus to our hotel in Antigua. The ride is long and by the time we arrive, it is dark. I catch him looking at me several times. He shakes his head and smiles, but doesn't say anything. He takes me up to the hotel room and excuses himself. When he returns, he picks up his bags. "I'll be down the hall," he says, as he walks out the door.

Several minutes later, as I'm still standing in my room wondering what to do next, he sends a text telling me to meet him for dinner in the hotel dining room, in an hour.

I shower and change into a short navy dress that shows my figure. Then decide I shouldn't push my luck and put on a pair of white trousers and a coral blouse that shows plenty of cleavage.

When I arrive in the dining room, Preston makes an obvious show of not looking at me. He keeps his eyes averted, his gaze directed just above my head.

"For Christ's sake!" I say. "Look at me!"

He relents and his gaze takes me in, traveling from my mouth to my cleavage.

"Am I such a monster?" I ask, leaning forward with a smirk.

"It isn't that. I just think it would be better if you hadn't survived."

"What?" I stare at him, hurt by his cold words. "You mean you wish I had died?"

I can't believe this is coming from a man I had spent so much time and effort trying to please. I love him and he wants me dead so much, he can't even keep it to himself. I am beginning to wonder what I see in him.

"Opal, it's been months... Laura and I have been moving on with our lives...as if you had died. This will..."

"I can't believe you!" I shout at him. "Laura wouldn't wish me dead."

"I wouldn't be so sure." He says and shakes his head, clearly angry again. "You look younger than your own daughter. How will that make her feel? Our entire family will be humiliated by what you've done to yourself."

"You mean you will be humiliated." I say.

He always did care more about appearances than how I felt. I don't even know why I am surprised by how he has responded to me.

He slumps in his chair. "I didn't realize how different you would look. I don't remember you being this pretty when you were younger. I mean, I can see you or...you look like a relative of yours."

"Which one?" I ask, sipping my margarita.

"That's not what I mean." He says, confused. "You look like someone in a younger generation who could be related to you; like a niece or a daughter."

"So, you don't find me attractive?" I ask.

"Every male in this place finds you attractive." He says, emphatically. "Every young man is thinking you are my daughter or a gold digger." He grins sardonically.

"I just want to go home, Preston. You have no idea how hard this has been living with all the physical pain, and the agony of being kept from my family and home. I want my life back."

Tears gather in my eyes and run down my cheeks.

"It's not a good idea." He refrains from looking at me. "Dr. Rushing said that you could cause lots of problems for the clinic if you return. You wouldn't want to do that, would you?"

"Dr. Rushing said that?" I ask. "You have been in touch with her?"

"Yes, she called to tell me you wanted to come home and that I needed to persuade you to stay with the rest of your kind." He glances up from his drink.

"My kind?" I knock over my water and though there isn't much in the glass, it heads straight for his lap. He quickly scoops up his napkin to stop the water.

"You know," he says, "the ones like you, who have those things inside them. She says you won't age and they aren't sure what you will really become."

I move closer to him. "What are you really afraid of Preston? That my youthfulness will embarrass *you*? That people will think less of *you*? Or are you afraid you might have feelings for me?"

"Opal," he pleads. "Understand that I am here to

negotiate with you on behalf of my family."

"You mean our family. Don't forget, I gave birth to our daughter."

"Our daughter," he concedes. "Our daughter doesn't expect you to survive. She has been told you are in a coma and that you may not survive."

"Who told her that?" I fume. "How can she believe that when she receives correspondence from me daily?"

"I did, because that is what I was led to believe." He spreads his hands begging. "Opal, we've all moved on. We've forced ourselves go forward without a chance of your returning." He looks down and sighs.

"What are you telling me?" My throat feels like it is closing and I can't catch my breath.

"I have found someone else who makes me very happy. I'm in love and I don't want you to ruin it for us. We didn't plan it, it just happened."

"We? Who is this person?" My heart pounds in my ears and the color drains from my face. I'm so afraid he will say the name that runs through my head. *Tess.*

"Tess."

"Oh." I shut down, close my eyes, and feel invisible. This couldn't have just happened. This little affair of theirs must have been going on while I was still in Nashville. "And this happened since I've been gone? Two months?"

"Opal, I'm happy for the first time in years. She has brought me back to life." His voice is soft and his face lights up as he talks. "Laura likes her and she fits into our little family. Look, we haven't been happy for years. We've tried to make it work."

I shoot anger out of my eyes. "No, Preston, I have worked on our marriage for years. You have done nothing but ignore me and our family. Don't pretend like you have done anything but push me away!" I stand up and push back my chair. I'm devastated. "I need to be alone," I say without looking at him. "I'm going back to my room."

Suddenly, I'm angry and I turn back to face him. "We *will* talk in the morning and you *will* do what I want. There will be no further discussion at this time!"

He stands as I turn and stalk off, but he doesn't try to call me back. I look back to see him drop into his seat defeated, tossing the wet napkin in his plate.

It is beyond me how he could engage in an affair with my best friend. I never thought he'd consider an affair, because Preston is so concerned about what others think. The fear of others finding out about it should have kept him faithful.

I crawl into bed and lay without thinking. I'm not hurt or angry anymore. I am totally numb. It seems like an eternity before I finally feel exhaustion taking over. I whisper one name before I drift off: "Tess."

⚘ ⚘ ⚘ ⚘ ⚘

In the morning, I don't have the answers I'd hope for. Both Tess and Preston thought I wouldn't survive, how could I blame them? I know Tess doesn't take falling in love lightly. She has affairs, but they don't last. She is always pushing men away. But how could she? They'd been told that I might die and I'm not dead.

Well, there isn't anything I can do about the two of them and how they feel about each other, but I refuse to step away from my daughter and granddaughter.

I don't meet with Preston in the morning, taking time, instead to think of plan for returning home without upsetting everyone's lives. I could fake my death and since I am a card-carrying organ donor; there won't be a body for burial. I could still return to Nashville, but as someone else… as my own niece. I don't really have a niece, but Laura doesn't know that, since she never met my brother, who died when she was very young. Nobody would question my niece having some resemblance to me. Preston can introduce me as Leslie Garmond, a twenty five-year-old cousin to my daughter who is in need of family support. That gives me a way to stay in the lives of my family and Preston will have to keep his mouth shut.

Satisfied with my plan, I make arrangements to meet

Preston and tell him. If he wants this, he will have to do it my way and depending on how my daughter reacts to the passing of her mother, I will judge for myself whether to reveal whom I really am.

Preston has always had his way in our marriage; I never had a say in anything. He uses intimidation by yelling and slamming doors; trying to make me afraid. It has always worked, but no more. If he wants to keep his new life peaceful, he'll do it my way.

⚘ ⚘ ⚘ ⚘ ⚘

"Absolutely not!" Preston is ranting as he paces the floor of my hotel room. "I will not be a part of this...this falsehood you are creating. You can't do this to me and my family!"

"Damn you! It's my family too. I didn't ask for this to happen to me, but you want to declare me dead and that's just as much a lie as this. I don't care if you want to play house with my ex-best friend, but you don't get to call all the shots anymore!"

"If you don't do this, I will come back there and run your lover out of our lives. She will leave, you know; if she knows I'm not dead. She doesn't like confrontation and will bow out of your life completely."

Preston's eyes widened. He looks like he believes every word I say. "Opal, you did this. This was your decision. You are suffering the consequences."

"Do I look like I'm suffering to you?" I laugh at him. "I'm not the little meek woman you married. You can't bully me into submission anymore, Preston." I cross my arms and gaze back at him with a satisfied smile.

"You can't do this." He pleads.

"I can and I am. Now do you still want to remain friends or do you want to make an enemy out of me?

"He sighs and sits on the bed defeated. "What do you want me to do with your stuff? Do you have any idea what kind of funeral you want?"

"Give all my jewelry to Laura except for the little ruby heart necklace that was my mother's. I want that. Clothes can go to charity. I do want the piano, my guitar, and all of my personal stuff...writing journals and jewelry-making supplies."

"How do you expect me to do that? Laura will have her hands in everything that is yours."

"You set it all up before you tell her I'm dead. Then you let her believe I disposed of all those things some months before I left for Switzerland."

As I look at him, I wonder how I could have loved this man for so long. He wishes I was dead and he's agreeing to just erase me from his life. I feel like our years together meant nothing to him.

"You will need to rent an apartment for me and you can

put my things in there along with my cookware, bake ware, and the few pieces of furniture I want." I hand him a list.

"You sure you want all your clothes to go to charity?" He asks.

"What, you think they will fit this body?" I gave my best seductive pose.

His eyes twinkle. "And what if Laura sees you have all her mother's things?"

"She won't feel comfortable enough to visit at first and she'll think her Daddy is very thoughtful to take care of Cousin Leslie." I smile, pleased with myself.

He rolls his eyes and shakes his head, but I see almost a hint of a smile. He is trying hard to stay angry. "I'm late." He says, glancing at his watch. "We will talk more when I get back from my trip." He turns to leave.

"Bye, Uncle Press!" I smile and wave sweetly.

He chuckles. "You're a real piece of work!"

"I'll take that as a complement! What, no goodbye kiss?"

He leans over and kisses my forehead.

"By the way, Damaris is taking you to the beach while Thomas and I are away. Be good!"

"I have a very sexy bikini. Want to see?"

He is laughing when he walks away.

I scored big today, but why do I feel sad? We actually

connected before he left. Can he still have feelings for me? We are still married and he is very desirable when he acts like this; playful and easygoing.

I miss passion and romance and long for deep kisses and being touched lovingly. It has been a long time since I've felt desired, since I've felt the heat of passion as it consumes me. I would love to rock someone's world when they look at me.

Preston and I haven't been good companions to one another the last few years. He sought out golf and fishing as his comforters. I wonder if our lives could have taken a different path if I had showed more interest in his hobbies. I can't berate myself anymore. I've read countless books and done some very self-demeaning things in an effort to get him to pay attention to me.

I thought that my age was ruining our marriage and that if I did something drastic like a facelift or liposuction that he would look at me differently. Now that I'm totally transformed, the truth is hard to face; he just doesn't love me anymore.

I walk over to the mirror and stare at myself. A ravishingly beautiful woman stares back at me…and he still doesn't want me.

"I give up!" I cry. My marriage is over.

CHAPTER 8

I stand on the beach, black sand blowing over my sandaled feet. The string bikini, that was a gift from Tess, doesn't cover much, but I am alone and enjoying this bit of sensuous freedom. I've never worn a bikini before, not even when I was a young girl, so the idea of being naughty and sultry appealed to the new rebellious side of me. Preston would never approve of so much exposed flesh—my flesh, so I revel in it.

The waves beckon to me with their promise of cool water that mists toward shore. I release my waist length blonde hair from the elastic band and let it blow around my head like a kite, that can't make up its mind which current of air to follow. I dip my toes in the lapping surf, testing its temperature. Cold. Very cold. I move away from the water, shivering as the breeze hits my wet feet. I don't stay cold long; the hot sun touches my skin and it prickles under the heat along my shoulders. I don't want to burn, so I sit back under the shade of the beach umbrella on a slatted chaise and rub sunscreen onto my legs.

I take deep breaths of the salty air, enjoying the briny smell that adds to the scene that holds me spellbound. I can hear voices wafting across the water from large party boats.

Watching squadrons of brown pelicans diving into the waves to fish, I take several pictures, while I observe their technique. Three or four will follow the waves and then fly down shore following more waves, while the ones up the beach will eventually make their way to where I rest. This is the first time I observe pelicans in the wild and I am pleased to capture them with my camera.

This beach is so quiet, with a primitive beauty—there is a profusion of flora everywhere with bougainvillea surrounding entire buildings, lending their bright pink and purple cover. Banana and lime trees grow in the black lava sand, along with the ever-present palms that spill up to the beach.

I close my eyes, listening to the sound of the surf and the wind singing its ocean lullaby, and fall asleep. When I wake, I stretch luxuriously and marvel that I lay flat on my back upon a wooden surface and didn't feel a bit of discomfort. Before the transformation, I hadn't slept on my back in twenty years and had felt pain in my shoulders every morning from sleeping on my side. This is freedom. I can feel the lubrication of my joints.

A noise to my left catches my attention and I realize I

am no longer alone on the beach. I quickly try to tidy my tangled hair, twisting it into a ponytail and stuffing it under my hat. I glance up to see who is occupying the bench next to me and find a man staring back at me. I feel the red blush surface on my cheeks and I rise to make my escape.

It's one thing to be on the beach in my scanty bikini by myself, but quite another to flaunt my body in the presence of a stranger. I was told this was usually a deserted beach, far from the fancy conveniences that most tourists demand, so I am surprised to find him here.

"Don't go," he reaches out his hand. "I'm sorry I startled you." His fingers are long and I can see thick calluses, the kind you see on guitar players.

He is dressed in cut off shorts and a t-shirt and wears a pair of Chucks without socks. His white teeth look brilliant in the tan face that smiles at me. My heart starts tapping out an SOS to my brain, but it has gone to the V between my legs instead. This guy is so hot! I've never had this type of response to a stranger before. The hunks at the gym were good to look at, but this guy is sex personified. He runs his fingers through his thick dark hair.

Wrapping my towel around myself, I continue gathering my beach gear and my camera. "No," I say. "I fell asleep and must get out of the heat. Please excuse me."

"You look like you could use a drink." He motions for

me to take the bottle of water he offers. "Please?" he asks. His kindness calms my fear.

I sit on the slatted bench and take the bottle of water. "Thank you," I say, looking at him sheepishly. "I am rather thirsty."

He looks embarrassed. "My name is Robbie Brand." He smiles a genuine smile, but looks like he is waiting for me to say something.

"I'm Opal," I say, removing my sunglasses to get a better look. "Are you staying at the hotel?"

"Not really," he says. "I'm at the resort at the other end of the beach. I just took a walk and ended up here." He looks like a cat that had swallowed a canary. Why would he look so guilty?

"Oh," I say, realizing that he probably stopped because he saw a nearly naked woman on the beach. I look around hoping to see someone else close by.

"Honestly," he says, "this area of the beach isn't usually used by tourists, so I was surprised to find you here. Um...I saw you in town yesterday and wanted to meet you. I don't have anyone to talk to and I don't speak Spanish very well, although, I understand more than I speak."

He seems very nervous, almost shy, and keeps looking up at me through his lashes. "Please, don't get me wrong. I don't mean you any harm. I'm just kind of lonely for someone to talk to."

I stare at him. His eyes are hazel with golden flecks surrounded by a darker blue ring. Long black eyelashes shade them and the thought "bedroom eyes" comes to mind. Several days' growth on his face and disheveled dark brown hair add to his scruffy charm. I guess his age to be late twenties or early thirties. And he has an accent that stirs hot in my core.

"You're English?" I ask.

He looks insulted. "I may be British," he grins, "but not English. I'm from Scotland."

"Are you vacationing?"

He spreads his arms wide and I notice a tattoo running up the inside of his arm, meeting his well-defined bicep that pulls at his shirtsleeve. "This country is so beautiful; so primitive." He laughs shyly. "Just a bit of an escape." He looks down and ends that last statement in a whisper, exhaling forcefully. "My life is hectic and I need some space to think...alone." He says, resigned as he rakes his fingers through his hair. This gesture seems to be his nervous tell. He looks sad. Maybe lonely.

"Well it was nice to meet you, Robbie," I say rising. "Perhaps I will see you around. Thanks for the water."

"Have dinner with me?" he asks rising. "Please? I don't want to face another evening meal alone."

I laugh. "But that's why you left- wherever you left. You

had to get away. This," I point at the beach, "is away!"

I wonder if he's trying to make me feel sorry for him on purpose. Play the sympathy card and then strike.

"Opal!" I hear my name being called and see Damaris running toward the beach.

"Damaris," I say stepping around the umbrella. "I'm here."

"Excuse me," I say to Robbie, tearing my eyes from his.

Damaris' face is anxious as she approaches. "What's wrong, Damaris? Have you heard from the guys?"

She is shaking her head and speaking quickly in Spanish. I only catch a few of the words, but not enough to get the message. "Damaris, I don't understand you."

"My sister and nephew were in an auto accident. I need to get to Belize. I called a taxi to take me to the airport. You must stay here and wait for Thomas and Preston. Alejandro, my brother will meet me at the airport and we will fly together." She is wringing her hands and silently crying. I know she feels very close to her nephew. She sees Robbie rise from his bench looking our way.

I take her arm leading her toward the hotel. "Don't worry about me, Damaris." I assure her. "I can take care of myself. Just go and see about your family. I'm sure your sister and Nephew will be just fine." My arms are around her, holding her tightly.

Damaris looks at my scantily clad body and smiles. "I can't get over how much you've changed from the last time we were together. You don't look like you are more than a teenager." Her eyes narrow. "Who is that man you were talking to?"

"I don't really know," I say, "just someone out for a walk on the beach."

"It scares me to leave you alone," she says with a worried look. "Who will take care of you? He is a foreigner; a very handsome foreigner."

"Damaris," I chide as we step into our room. "I may look like a child, but remember that I am two years older than you. I can take care of myself."

"But you can't speak the language very well and what will Thomas say if I leave you alone?" She looks genuinely worried.

"Please, Damaris. Just go. Your sister needs you and your taxi is here."

She picks up her suitcase and runs to the door. "Don't take chances Opal, be safe. I will call my friends and ask them to check on you."

"I will be fine," I reassure her and push her towards the taxi, honking with impatience.

"Just go. Call me when you get there and let me know how your sister is doing."

She waves from the taxi.

I close the hotel door and pull the blinds. I don't know if Mr. Gorgeous is still on the beach or not, but what I need is a shower and a change of clothes. I step into the bathroom and turn on the faucet, remembering that it takes a while for the water to get hot. I stare at my reflection in the mirror behind the door. I still can't get over my new appearance. The younger me looks back from a body with skin that glows all peachy cream, with a tint of sun.

The saying "*I wish I was able to go back to my youth and know what I know now*" makes me laugh out loud. Physically I am twenty-three, but I have the experience of a middle-aged woman. To think that I was so attractive to a man so young as the one I just met on the beach makes me shiver, as I step into the warm water.

After my shower, I lounge on the bed, contemplating my next few days alone. I don't mind being alone in Nashville, but being a single woman alone in a country where she doesn't speak the language is frightening. It would be different if I was still in my original birthday suit, but this new body brought its own brand of danger.

I'm not oblivious to the stares from men. Many look at me like they stare at centerfolds. It still surprises me because when I think about *me*, I see myself as the old me in the old body. Will I ever completely get used to the new packaging?

What was it the hazel-eyed hunk had said? He had seen me in town? That was exactly the kind of thing I wanted to avoid. This man actually came looking for me. Had he followed Damaris and me to the hotel last night? He seemed nice enough and I don't feel any distress when I talk to him--however briefly. Usually I can sense danger, but I didn't with Robbie.....Rand? Sand? What did he say his last name was? He is so handsome with that rugged outdoorsy look. My insides quiver. I catch myself imagining what it would be like to have him hold me close and run my hands over his tattoo.

The room is cool and the bed comfortable, so I easily drift off for a nap. I wake several hours later to a loud crashing noise. My heart races until I see that the wind is whipping across the sand and has knocked over a metal rubbish bin. The sun is low in the sky and I decide to have an early dinner.

As I leave the hotel room, I realize just as the door clicks closed, that I've left without my key. Now what? No key. I stop by the front desk, but there is a sign on the desk "The office will be closed this evening, sorry for the inconvenience." I walk out to the lanai, but it's empty except for a blanket and pillow on the lounge chair. I may just have to sleep here if the office isn't open when I return from dinner.

The small restaurant I like isn't far away and I feel safe walking there from the hotel. Just as I come around to the front of the hotel, a couple I met yesterday pull into the drive.

"Opal?" The woman asks.

"Yes," I answer with a smile.

"Maybe you remember me; Stephanie. Damaris introduced us last night." She doesn't wait for my answer. "She phoned me before leaving this afternoon. Isn't it horrible about her sister? Anyway," she went on, "she asked us to see that you have some company for dinner tonight. Please, join us."

Her husband jumps out of the car and opens the back door, helping me up into their Jeep. The ride to the restaurant is jarring; the car swerves but seems to hit every pothole along the way. I rode an elephant once and this ride is not unlike that, except that it doesn't smell.

"Thank you so much for asking me," I say gratefully." I was going to try to walk there, but I can see now that it would have been dangerous. There aren't many lights between the hotel and restaurant and the condition of the stone roads make it almost impossible to navigate."

"You mustn't be so foolish. Guatemala is beautiful, but it is a third-world country and can be very dangerous for foreigners. Just last night there were three home invasions in well-to-do neighborhoods." Garrett informed me.

"Maybe you should come and stay with us until Damaris returns." Stephanie turns in her seat looking at me earnestly. "It's just for a few days and then you can go back to the beach."

"I wouldn't want to intrude," I say.

"Oh, please," Stephanie laughs. "You know we have many boarders at the plantation. We can make room for one more."

"Can you put me to work?" I ask, suddenly inspired. They live in the midst of the most beautiful coffee plantation I had the pleasure of touring on the last trip Preston and I took to Guatemala. I found it enchanting. "I would love to help you at the gift shop or something." I say.

"I think that would be a marvelous idea," she pacifies me. "If you are sure that is what you want to do. You are here on vacation. I will take you riding in the morning."

They owned beautiful horses, but I hadn't been on a horse in years. My first thought is about my injured back, but then, giggling to myself, I remember that I don't have an injured back anymore.

"That will be great fun!"

CHAPTER 9

Loud music flows into the street from the restaurant and I'm glad that we have finally arrived. I don't relish the trip back to the hotel, remembering I've locked myself out of my room. I wait until we are seated and explain to my new friends about my situation.

The restaurant is simply gorgeous. It looks like nothing from the outside. Just stuccoed walls with peeling white wash and a huge old wooden door with large iron strips holding the planks together, hung on big iron hinges.

You feel the cool air before you step inside and the wonderful smell of flowers, herbs, and fresh made tortillas draw you deeper through the shaded entrance to the lantern-lit interior. Trees with red and blue macaws on perches and hanging flowers make a kaleidoscope of colors that contrast with the heavy old wood of the balconies and curving staircases.

This had been a very old residence at one time and is now a hotel and restaurant. The kitchen is in the open and you can watch the cooking process and see the women making the tortillas. They are dressed in the traditional clothes of the

Guatemalan tribes, with the matching headdresses.

"So, I locked myself out of my room right before I left." I spread my hands and shrug my shoulders. "I am going to sleep on the lanai tonight and hopefully the hotel office will be open again in the morning."

"You have your purse with you. Is there anything else of value you don't want to leave?" Stephanie asks. "Garrett knows the owner of the hotel. He can call him and ask for another key." She turned to Garrett. "Actually, Garrett, we should really get her things tonight, so she can stay with us. Why don't you call him now."

Garrett rises from the table, phone in hand and walks to a quiet corner of the restaurant. He returns just as our drinks arrive.

"Mr. Rojas said he would leave a key for you under the flower pot on the left side of the lanai. I explained the situation and he apologized for your inconvenience. He will keep your reservation open until Thomas returns." He smiles. "See, no problemo." He laughs and takes a sip of his margarita.

Stephanie and Garrett get up to dance. I watch as they gracefully move to a Meringa beat. Garrett has a scowl on his face when he looks my way, as if I am an enemy or a bug to be crushed. I look behind me to see that there is no one there. The look was definitely for me. What I could have done to offend him? Perhaps he doesn't like unexpected guests.

I motion to Stephanie that I am going to look around. The sun is setting and the flower garden is lit with a profusion of Chinese lanterns and candles. It is breathtaking. I sit on a bench admiring the view and breathing in the sweet smell of jasmine and gardenia. Someone is smoking a cigar. I can smell its slight musky tobacco scent.

My mind drifts back to the beach and the hazel eyes that are always there when I close mine. A shiver of delight runs through me.

"Hello," a man whispers in my ear. "Do you mind?" he says sitting down next to me. His thigh is against mine as he squeezes onto the small bench under a tree. He is in a dark suit with a white shirt open at his throat. His cologne is subtle, but somewhat familiar, and makes me want to take more breaths. It mellows the sweet smell of the flowers.

He smiles and chuckles lightly. "I can tell by your expression that I didn't make much of an impression on you this afternoon."

I look up into hazel eyes and blink twice trying to clear my head, but the eyes are still there. "You look different." I smile. "Robbie isn't it? You clean up nice!" I am actually happy to see him. Tingles run up my arm as he holds the hand I offer him.

His face is clean-shaven and his hair gleams, still slightly disheveled, but very sexy. His smile brings out slight dimples that make me swoon. My head starts spinning and I am forgetting something. Ah yes, to breathe.

"I must say you look beautiful every time I see you." His eyes twinkle. "You simply took my breath away this afternoon."

My face flushes. "I wasn't expecting an audience." I say.

I sense or hear a strange humming. It feels like a cord or an invisible wire linking us together. Maybe it's an electrical conduit because I hear it buzzing inside me. Suddenly, I realize he is still talking, so it must be going on inside of me or he surely would say something.

"I couldn't help overhearing about your friend's sister. Have you heard from her?" He asks, concerned. His eyes sweep down to my thighs and back up to take in my breasts. He isn't bashful about what he wants, as his gaze lands on mine and his message is pure desire.

"No," I say. "She hasn't contacted me, yet. Thank you for asking. That is very kind of you."

He smiles. "Well, I am here at the request of some old friends of mine and I'm late." He rises to leave. "Perhaps we will meet again, Opal." He stands and I run my gaze over his hair and down his face, looking into his mesmerizing eyes.

"Yes," I say shaking my head. "That would be nice."

We walk back to the tables together and find to our surprise that we both joined Stephanie and Garrett. Stephanie begins the introductions.

"Opal, this is a friend of ours. His name is probably familiar to you. Robbie Brand. He is um... from Scotland."

She is looking at him strangely and I look up in time to see him motioning to her. There is something about him he doesn't want her to tell me.

"Robbie," she says, turning to me. "This is Opal Sanders."

"Actually," I say, smiling "We met this afternoon on the beach."

Stephanie looks at Robbie surprised. "Really?"

Garrett twists his pursed lips. "Well, then, we can dispense with the introductions." He turns to Robbie. "What will you have to drink?"

"Pineapple juice will do fine, thank you." His eyes meet mine and hold them until Stephanie interrupts.

"Robbie, you didn't tell me you had met anyone this afternoon." She says waiting for his explanation.

"It was a brief encounter, Stephanie." He explains. "I didn't know if I would ever see Opal again." He looks at me and smiles and I know then that he would have found a way.

I wonder what he will think of me when he discovers that I am married and that my husband is sixty-six years old. Gold digger? I'm sure that would fit his description. I don't know why I am so worried what he thinks. After all, he's a young man and I'm probably just another pretty girl to him. He would be shocked if he found out my age, that I am a grandmother, and have been married for thirty-five years. That will send him running away as fast as he can. The mental picture makes me laugh.

"What's funny," he asks, still gazing at me.

"Something I just remembered," I say, smiling as I turn to the waiter who sets plates full of hot food in front of us.

"Opal, you're too quiet," Garrett looks at me sternly. "You need to talk more.

Stephanie quickly asks a question. "Damaris told me you have started a jewelry business. Do you design the pieces or just sell to other designers?"

I smile at her. "I design them myself. I have a few pieces with me I can let you see."

I am thankful she stopped Garrett. I am sure he is going to ask about my husband. That would end my private joke. Although, I am beginning to feel that the joke is on me. I don't want Robbie to know about me. I want to continue to pretend that what he sees, is what I am; a young, single woman. And why not? My marriage is over, after all. I suddenly feel sad.

Robbie asks me to dance after the dinner dishes are removed and the coffee is brought to the table. His hand guides me to the floor and he lightly pulls me into his arms. I feel butterflies in my stomach and think I will be sick. I can feel the heat coming from his hand on my back. I feel foolish, after all, I'm not an ingénue and I'm still married.

But, this is something I crave; the newness of a romance; the promise of excitement. My husband has made it clear that he's moved on and has no desire to be with me. Don't I deserve the passion that every woman longs for? Isn't that why women of all ages read romance books?

"You are a million miles away from here," Robbie breathes in my ear, sending a tiny tingle into my shoulders and running down my spine, causing my knees to wobble.

"I'm sorry; I guess I'm just thinking of Damaris." I lie.

I look up into those hazel eyes. Wow. I am lost in them. I have to end this infatuation soon. I don't want to have any type of relationship based on lying, especially to myself. What am I thinking? Didn't I just make plans to deceive Laura and Lucy? Why can't I just enjoy what life brings my way?

He continues looking at me. I lick my lips and his eyes lock onto them. There is a current of some type running back and forth between us. I am worried it will make permanent bonds. I look down and step away from him.

"Whoa" I say dizzily. I take a deep breath.

"You feel that?" he asks.

I look around. It seems everyone has felt the same blast of current. Some people are smoothing their hair and rubbing their arms. "Thank you for the dance," I say glancing up at him.

He wears a smirk and chuckles softly. "Anytime, Opal." His hand never leaves my back as we exit the dance floor.

We make small talk the rest of the evening. He keeps his secrets and I keep mine. He pulls my chair out when it is time to go and gives me his arm to steady myself. Once again, the current running through us seems to discharge around us, causing bulbs to burst. I can't look away from Robbie's eyes, or he mine.

Garrett finally catches our attention with a loud cough. Flustered, I let go of his arm and follow Garrett and Stephanie. I don't even say goodnight.

I find the key at the hotel and pack my belongings. Garrett stashes them in the Jeep. We discuss the current that ran through the restaurant. Stephanie thinks it is something that cannot be explained naturally. When she says that when soul mates meet it is supposed to garner a supernatural magnetic pull, I scoff.

"Whaaat?" she asks incredulously. "You don't believe in soul-mates? I was once told by my grandmother that there is always the man you love, the man who loves you, and the man you marry. When these three men are all one and the same, you have found your soul mate. Many times women love men they can't have, or a man loves you, but you don't love him. Women marry men they don't love all the time. They are afraid they won't ever be asked for their hand in marriage and marry the first man who asks. Sometimes women marry for financial stability or pedigree. Marrying for love is passé these days."

"Now, I am an exception. With you darling, Garrett," she says taking his hand. "I have found my soul mate."

Garrett Laughs. "You have more crazy beliefs than the oldest grandma alive," he says carrying my bags and following Stephanie upstairs at the coffee farm.

She makes a face at him, shows me to my room, and says good night. I leave the unpacking until the morning and venture onto the balcony to drink in the moonlight and the scent of night-blooming jasmine. This is a night for romance. Too bad Preston is away. Then I remember; he doesn't want me anyway.

I sigh and think of those intoxicating hazel eyes. Infatuation, I warn myself. Get a grip and stop fanaticizing about that young man. He will only reject you when he discovers your secret. Imagine how he will feel about having a fifty-six year old woman. He is young and vibrant and wants a woman who is able to experience life with him. He wouldn't like being deceived.

I shouldn't be sad. I have a new body and a new life to look forward to. I have a wonderful daughter and divine granddaughter and I'm loved by both of them. I just don't have the right to wish for more. My wishes are all fulfilled and I have the new body to prove it.

Be careful what you wish for—my conscience betrays my fears.

Now, I don't seem to fit in anywhere. I'm too young for my "Silver-Sneakers" friends at the gym and too old for people the same age as my new body. I didn't ask for this; I only wanted to make myself look ten years younger, not thirty. Now I won't be aging at all–the clinicians don't know how long I'll live. They call me an imMEMortal.

CHAPTER 10

I awake in the morning to the sound of roosters crowing. There is knock on my door, as I emerge from the bathroom dressed in jeans and a long-sleeved white cotton shirt. I pull my hair up into a ponytail high on my head and looped around itself several times, which makes it shorter and more manageable.

Stephanie is waiting for my answer and she is happy to see I am dressed and ready to go. "Bring a hat and sunscreen." she calls back over her shoulder. "It will help to have a pair of sunglasses also. The sun bouncing off the ocean is blinding!"

I pick up a baseball hat and pull my ponytail through the hole in the back. My sunglasses are already in my hand and the sunscreen in the beach bag.

I wonder if we are going to get any breakfast before we leave. To my surprise, Stephanie has packed a picnic.

"Coffee?" she asks holding up a paper coffee cup.

"You bet!" I brighten instantly. A prickly sensation starts in my back and work its way up my scalp. I turn, but don't see anything. Maybe the nanites are doing something. It feels like that invisible cord started again, but suddenly left.

We take our coffee and make our way to the stables. The horses are tacked up and ready to ride. It seems that horseback riding is like bike riding—one never forgets how to ride.

We have a wonderful time riding down the beach. The air is clean and the spray from the surf, thrown into the air by the horse's hoofs, sparkles in the sun like diamonds throwing rainbows all around us. My pant legs and shoes are drenched, but we laugh and ride until we reach a little inlet where we follow the creek into the woods and up the side of a steep hill.

Stephanie finally pulls her horse to a stop and dismounts near a natural small amphitheater-like area. She spreads a cloth on the ground and unloads the picnic onto two stoneware plates. There is a nice fruit salad with pineapple, bananas, papaya, coconut, and mango. Tortillas are rolled up with black beans and sliced beef topped with a few pickled onions and a piquant Salsa Verde for dipping. There are slices of avocado and tomato drizzled with olive oil and fresh herbs. It is delicious and very satisfying.

Stephanie lowers her plate and looks at me intently. "Now," she begins, "I want to know why a young girl like you would want some old crony. Is it the money?" She is not angry, but close to it. "I mean, you have your youth and beauty."

I hold up my hand and put my head down slightly looking at her through my eyelashes. I'm not ashamed, but I don't want to see her rejection. "So you've met my husband?"

"Stephanie," I start. "I guess Damaris didn't tell you about my transMEM. At least, that is what I like to call it." I shouldn't tell anyone, Dr. Rushing told me to keep it secret, but I really like Stephanie and don't want her to think badly of me. "I am older than you, actually—at least chronologically. Physically, I will remain twenty-three for many years."

"What?" she looks confused. Her face flushes.

"I saw an ad for stem-cell rejuvenation or anti-aging procedure in Switzerland. Usually the process rejuvenates the skin and underlying tissues to erase ten or fifteen years. In my case, it mixed with my DNA and rejuvenated by entire body."

I smooth my napkin looking down. I don't feel right talking about the nanites. "It has caused many problems for me with my marriage and in my life in general."

"I have been married to Preston for thirty-five years and I'm really fifty-six years old. However, my husband is having an affair with my best friend and he wants to declare me dead and have nothing more to do with me." I wipe away a few tears.

She looks at me incredulously. "What the hell are you crying for? You have been given the greatest gift anyone could receive." She reaches out to grasp my hand. "Your skin is so soft," she says. "Don't tell me Preston isn't pleased."

"Believe me, he is anything but pleased."

We are both silent for some time, listening to the brilliant wildlife around us. In the distance, I can hear the ocean waves hitting the shore, the buzzing of bees in the sweet smelling flowers, and unusual birdcalls. The horses snort and it is so quiet in our little sanctuary, I can hear them chewing.

"It wasn't an easy transformation, you know," I explain. "I had all kinds of problems and was in the clinic for several months until the age-reversal slowed. Losing my teeth was the last and final act of cruelty." I sneered with the memory. "Of course new ones grew in their place, but it was pure torment. Imagine growing twenty-six new teeth in a few weeks."

Stephanie shakes her head. "What will you do?" she asks. "I mean when everyone you know is gone?"

"I don't even allow myself to think of that," I say. "I can't think of that." My eyes fill up with tears again. "My doctor seems to think I should find new relationships to help me along the way and now that Preston has moved on, I can allow myself to fall in love again."

"That husband of yours is a prick and you are a glutton for punishment if you try to keep him in your life. Love is knocking at your door. Don't you think Robbie is gorgeous?"

I sigh. "Robbie is very hot! Do you mean to tell me he doesn't have women throwing themselves at him? He could have any woman he wants with just a smile."

She laughs. "I don't think Robbie wants an affair and I

think he is totally smitten with you. Yesterday, he was talking about this woman he had seen in town and said he was ready to settle down, if he could convince her to marry him."

I look aghast. "Marry him? I don't even know him. Nor does he know me. What do you think he would say about marrying a fifty-six year old woman?" I wonder if she was one of his women at one time. "Did you and he…?"

"Heavens no! He's like a son to me. I don't think your age would bother him; I wouldn't write him off yet. He is really a pretty decent guy. The limelight hasn't tainted his morals, nor has he had any drug related problems. I believe he did have a bit of a drinking problem when he was younger, but he doesn't touch alcohol anymore. Which is really saying something for someone with his fame?"

"Fame?" I ask.

Stephanie looks startled. "Oh, no! He asked me not to say anything." She is very upset. "Please don't let on I told you this; he is a lead singer with a very famous alternative band." She smiles. "Being fifty-six, you probably haven't been exposed to that type of music. I know I hadn't, but then I don't live in the States anymore."

"You seem to know him well. How did that happen?"

"Um…he has been here several times when he needs a safe haven to get away from his adoring fans and the paparazzi," she says.

I watch her when she talks about Robbie, the way her pupils dilate and she looks like she is going into a trance; with a little satisfied smile that plays around her lips. I've seen that look before on parents who are proud of their children. She is definitely more than a friend.

"Will you live forever?" she returns to me.

"The doctors don't know how long I'll keep regenerating." I answer. "Thank you for your ear and your concern. You cannot imagine how hard it is for me to share this."

I stare at her. She doesn't look much older than me, although she's wearing quite a bit of makeup. She is younger than she pretends to be. Her hair is bleached white and she keeps it in an older bouffant style that also lends to her mask. I pull her hand into the light. "You don't look much older than me," I say. "What are you playing at?"

"Shhhh!" she hushes me. "Keep your voice down."

"What?" I draw her closer. "You are like me, aren't you?" I ask, releasing her hand.

"Yes," she whispers. "It happened about thirty-five years ago. I was in Switzerland for about five years when I decided to try Dr. Englesteine's procedure. It was new then and there were many complications and half transformations. Many of the experimental projects failed—at the expense of the people who trusted the doctors."

She looks angry. "I too had the total transformation, but I am aging now. Not quickly, but it is happening. I was in my early twenties at the start of my new life and now I'm in my mid-thirties."

She looks at me. "Don't you feel that this transformation is cheating you out of your life? I mean, my first husband died and now I have Garrett." She smiles. "Darling Garrett. I wouldn't trade him for the world, but we stay the same and life passes us by." Tears drop from her cheeks into her lap.

"Did you know what I was last night?" I ask.

"Sylvia Rushing contacted me and told me that someone would be making a trip to Antiqua. She asked me to try to keep an eye out for you." Stephanie confesses. "I just didn't know you would be dropping into my lap." She smiles. "I'm really glad. I've been lonely for the others. I lived with them for many years before meeting Garrett and moving to the coffee farm. It's lovely here." She sighs.

"So," I counter, "why did you pretend not to know?"

"I have to be careful." She says. "As I said, there are others and they...don't like us very much."

I must look shocked and frightened by what she's said.

"Don't worry; I don't think they are in Guatemala."

"But why and who are they? If you're not worried why are you scared?"

"As I said, there are those whose operations didn't go well and they're different. I really think they might be crazy, like maybe their brains are jumbled."

"They won't hurt us, will they? Aren't we victims as well?"

"Honey, you don't look like a victim of anything. You look like an angel. Now that I know, I can see that glow in your skin," she says turning my hand over. "Brighter than I've ever seen."

"I had feathers one day." I offer, smiling.

"What? Really?"

"Yes," I laugh. "I dreamed I was a white bird one night and woke up with feathers."

She looks skeptical.

"Not real feathers. They were made from dry skin and disintegrated when touched."

"How did that happen?" She asks.

"The nanites. I had some trouble with them for a while. They can read my thoughts and created neural pathways—they evolved."

"No wonder you had trouble getting away from Dr. Rushing. She would definitely want to keep you under lock and key." She shakes her head. "Don't trust that woman!"

I don't talk for some time and just keep pulling at the grass.

"She scares me a bit, but I am really at her mercy. I don't know what to do. I keep having all kinds of problems. Imagine having a bunch of machines that keep acting out your dreams and desires."

"That would be horrible!" She says.

"It's better now, though. I convinced them to leave my body."

"Really? All of them?"

"I can't be positive, but I think so. I haven't had any more episodes." Better to keep up the lie assuming that Stephanie is reporting to Dr. Rushing.

She repacks the picnic and we rise to leave. "Do you think that means you will age normally?"

"I don't know; maybe, if they are all gone."

"Stay with us for a few months. I'll keep you busy. Let your husband go home and arrange your funeral. Take time to fall in love with Robbie." She blushes. "If not Robbie, then somebody else. You could at least have an affair."

I laugh. "I like you Stephanie. You might be good for me!"

We mount the horses and return to the stables. I take another tour of the coffee plantation and have a swim in the pool. It seems that I can't give up the late afternoon nap. I close the wooden shutters to block out the sun and rest until it is time to go down to dinner. I dress in a simple yellow, silk sheath dress.

Standing on the balcony overlooking the flower gardens, I can smell the Datura's hypnotic scent and inhale deeply. There is also a light masculine scent in the air, one I am already acquainted with...and the telltale hum that follows it.

CHAPTER 11

Robbie steps out into the garden and walks around the fountain, turning to look straight at me. I feel the pull of his sexy smile immediately; it leaves me melting and my inside quivering. Like a bee to honey, I am irresistibly drawn to him. So are several other women I spot as they make their way to his side. He turns to give each one his full attention. Two women take his arms as he leads them to the dining room, while another follows behind.

Well, what did you expect? I ask myself. He is handsome and single and evidently, he is a rock star with no shortage of admirers who would willingly be his next conquest.

I lock my room and leave to meet Stephanie for dinner. When I appear at the bottom of the stairs, Robbie disentangles himself from his entourage and steps towards me. "Excuse me ladies." He throws over his shoulder. "This is my date."

"You are absolutely stunning!" He says to me as he offers me his arm and kisses my cheek. There's that humming again. "Huh. What is that?" He mumbles to himself.

Stephanie and Garret are already seated, but Robbie steers me over to a secluded table. "And in candlelight you are glowing." His eyes sweep over my hair and end at my lips. "If I didn't know better, I would say you were an angel."

"You're not so bad yourself." I manage to say. "I believe you broke several hearts just now."

He dismisses my comment with a shrug.

"What would you like to drink?" He asks, seeing that the waiter has arrived.

"A Gimlet would be fine."

His eyes narrow, but he smiles. "That's an old fashioned drink for such a young woman!"

I wince, realizing I may have just revealed my age. "I like the taste of gin and lime."

He orders mango juice.

I tell him that Stephanie accidently let it slip that he is the lead singer in the band, Inventing Abbey. He rolls his eyes. We stare at each other before he gives me that wry smile of his.

"So, you really haven't heard my name before?" He seems shocked.

"No. Sorry. I'm not up on new music. I'm from Nashville, Tennessee and although I'm not a real country music fan, I have written a few songs that have been recorded."

"Really?" He seems surprised.

"Yes, but I was much younger then." I goof again. Why can't I keep my mouth shut? It won't work for me to pretend with Laura if I couldn't sustain the lie for longer than five minutes.

"How much younger could you have been? What did you do, write the songs when you were five?" He laughs.

"Can we talk about something else? I don't like talking about me. What are you doing here at the coffee farm?"

"But how can I get to know you if we can't talk about you. I want to learn as much about you as I can." Robbie looks serious. "Now that we have met, I'm never letting you go."

"Whoa," I breathe. "Much too fast!"

He ignores my protest and stands up, leading me to the dance floor and taking me in his arms. "This doesn't feel right to you?" His eyes stare into mine. He lowers his head and lightly touches my lips with his. "This doesn't feel right to you?"

His lips are soft on mine, my head is spinning, and I can't breathe.

He notices. "Breathe, Opal."

"Yes." I shudder breathlessly.

He takes me back towards the table and picks up our drinks. "Let's take a walk," he says as he guides me out the back of the restaurant. We sit on a bench near the fountain under the stars. I faintly hear the music and the general noise of the restaurant.

I know he is staring at me, so I turn. My heart is erratic and beating loudly in my ears. I swallow a bit of gin and cough, setting the drink aside. "Strong," I say.

Robbie places his arm around me and draws my head to rest on his shoulder. I can actually hear his heart racing too.

"Do you believe in love at first sight?" He whispers.

"I believe in laws of attraction." I lean away from him, looking into his eyes. The moon glows bright gold and the clouds surrounding it gleam like a halo. I can see them reflect in his eyes.

He suddenly shifts his gaze to me and I am looking into a pool of forbidden desires that I know will suck me down, take root, and blossom forth with destructive consequences.

I turn away from him. "Robbie, I don't know what is happening, but I can't get involved with anyone. I'm here trying to get over someone."

I am certain this is just his pickup technique.

"I'm patient." His hand reaches out for mine. "I'm not letting you go. I'll wait." He insists. The hum increases as he reaches up to cup my chin, turning my face back to his and looking into my eyes.

"You will?" I ask.

His voice, his touch, and his smile take my breath away,

again. I can feel that smoldering look paralyzing every excuse to run from him. I am no longer able to turn away. "Breathe, Opal." He whispers again, chuckling with a masculine tenor that makes my heart pump faster.

I take a deep breath and start laughing. "You can't look at me like that."

His mouth finds mine and crushes me in a river of desire. One hand cups the back of my head as he deepens his kiss, his tongue circling my lips, then parting them to seek mine. I finally stop resisting and surrender to the assault on my senses. The taste of him explodes my world. I wrap my arms around his neck, bringing him closer then quickly end the kiss, lowering my head against his chest.

Robbie is winded also; his breathing near my ear drives me crazy. He makes small kisses from my ear to my throat and back to my mouth that finds his in hungry passion. I run my fingers through his hair and he groans.

Robbie stands, drawing me to my feet and we dance a slow dance wrapped in each other's arms. I can feel his rising need, as he moves his hand to my lower back and pulls me tight against him, his lips kissing my neck and moving up again to lock on my mouth.

"Opal," He whispers with desire. "I don't know if I can control this need for you." He steps away. My nipples are rock hard and he doesn't miss how they strain against the thin silk material of my dress.

I pull him back, kissing his neck and nibbling on his ear lobe. He brings my face back to his and looks into my eyes, drawing me into his soul. My insides are weak and I'm shaking with desire.

He kisses the end of my nose and embraces me in a tight hug. He buries his nose in my neck. "You smell delicious. I will make you forget this other man!"

"Robbie," I whisper his name and push him away gently. Somehow, I walk to our table with his hand in mine. He sits opposite me, and smiles.

I can still taste Robbie's kisses and it is all I can do to keep from dragging him from the restaurant and up the stairs to my room. I release several large breaths and watch Robbie smile.

"Okay," he starts, "tomorrow, we will go zip-lining. We'll keep it friendly and stay around other people."

"What is zip-lining?"

"You'll see. Think roller coaster, without the coaster." He explains, laughing.

"Sounds terribly exciting," I say. "I'm all for something dangerous."

His arm snakes across the table and grabs my hand. The look on his face is sensual. "I can be dangerous if you want." He winks and his thumb strokes over the knuckles on the hand he holds.

"I bet you could." There goes my breathing again. "Quit looking at me like that!"

He shakes his head. His dimples deepen when he throws his head back and laughs.

"You should be used to women going gaga over you. Don't you have groupies?"

"Not me. I don't stick around to meet them." He motions to the waiter to bring our dinner. "I did the first couple of years, but it got old quickly. And although it isn't popular, I have been longing for a meaningful relationship for a while. The only woman in my life now is Stephanie and she is like a mother hen."

"And all the other women who want to be friends? Were those other women your body guards or harem?" I ask.

"They mean nothing. So who is this guy you are trying to forget?"

"Who says I'm trying to forget him? I believe I said get over him. I can never forget him." I say cryptically.

He looks confused. "Aren't they the same?"

"It's complicated. Robbie," I start. "You don't know me. I don't know you. We should take the time to get to know one another."

"You don't believe in love at first sight? Soul mates? This is how forever after love begins," he says emphatically.

"I've seen you a total of three times and already I can't separate my life from yours. We hum when we are near each other. I feel it and I know you do too."

I study Robbie over my coffee. Men don't proclaim such feelings on a first date. He must be full of it, and yet he sounds sincere. I could use this infatuation to thrust myself into the world of simple one-night stands and enjoy what fate brings my way, but I have never been an easy lay. I am a woman who enjoys serious relationships, or think I do. I've only dated three men in my life and only had sex with one.

"You are scaring me. I am not used to moving this fast," I say. This has to be his line to get me in bed, doesn't it?

"Okay," he says resigned. "But, I will wait."

"I want you to wait, but it isn't right of me to ask you to do that." I can play his game. I stand up and push back my chair. "I'm going to my room. I enjoyed your company. See you in the morning?"

"Come," he says taking my hand. "I'll walk you to your room."

"I don't think that is a good idea."

"I'll be a gentleman, if you really want me to."

His goodnight kiss is soft and quick. I watch as he walks away. When he turns the corner down the hall, I shut the door and the humming stops.

I step onto the balcony and watch him walk out to the

front parking area. He stops and speaks to the same women I saw him with earlier. One of them pulls him in close and plants a kiss on his lips. He walks away laughing at something she says. Yeah, he's a player.

I lie awake for hours, obsessing over my feelings for Robbie. This is what I have been longing for and now that it's within my grasp, I'm terrified and I'm pushing it away.

Should I just treat this as a fling? Maybe enjoy myself for a few weeks before I return to Laura and Lucy? Robbie will forget me after it's over, knowing my secret may be just the thing to put him off. How can I even trust the things he was saying? He could be the greatest manipulator on the planet. He can't be hurting for lovers. I'm sure any number of women would fall for those eyes, that accent, and those kisses.

Sometime during the night, I finally fall asleep. It is past nine in the morning when I finally wake. I quickly dress in a pair of shorts and a sleeveless blouse. I put on my hiking boots, pull my hair back in a braid, and stick it through the hole at the back of my baseball cap. I grab a small satchel I bought in Switzerland and toss my phone, camera, and sunglasses inside.

Stephanie and Robbie are nowhere to be seen when I enter the dining room so I order an espresso, a croissant, and tropical fruit salad.

I feel the hum before Robbie makes his presence

known and walks to my table.

"Morning sweetness," he leans down and kisses my cheek. "Ready for our dangerous adventure?"

"Oh God, if you are going zip-lining, you shouldn't have eaten so much," Stephanie interjects.

"She'll be okay. We'll walk down by the ocean for a few hours first," he says.

Robbie takes my hand in his and kisses it. "Come on Opal, let's go explore the beach."

"You look tired," he says, touching the dark circles under my eyes.

"Your fault," I say.

"My fault? I left your virtue intact."

"Yeah, but I thought about you all night long." I smirk.

He chuckles. "Don't worry," he says, "I didn't get much sleep either. I swam until after 1:00 a.m."

"Do you think this is a good idea?"

"I think we will just have to 'break-in' the relationship." He laughs and kisses my hand again. I lean forward and hug him. "Keep that up and I'll need another dip in the pool."

We walk hand in hand through the farm following the path to the beach. He introduces me to all the horses; by name. They are named after movie star couples like George and Gracie, Fred and Ginger, Princess Leia and Han Solo, and Scarlett and Rhett.

Taking our shoes off and tying the laces together so we could carry them, we walk through the tide, chatting and laughing like two old friends. Soon we come upon an outcropping of rocks and sit to enjoy the misty spray. He takes a small tube of sunscreen out of his pocket and proceeds to rub some on my arms and face.

"You shouldn't burn such beautiful cheeks," he says. "or this cute little nose; or this chin." His kiss is gentle and tender. "There, you won't burn." He puts the cream away.

My insides are quivering. His touch, his manly musk, his muscular body, the way he tastes, and his deep rich voice send ribbons of vibrations directly to my sex.

"Opal, are you breathing?" He chuckles.

I exhale, blowing the air forcefully out of my mouth.

I put my arms around him and lean my head against his back. I can feel his tight abs and his muscular chest. "Mmm. I think I could sleep like this."

He puts his arms over mine and holds my hands. The current between us hums. It is a constant when he is around and makes me feel content. We sit like this for some time before he opens my arms and stands, offering me his hands to help me up. Jumping down from the rocks, we start back the way we came.

Robbie is silent as we walk.

"A dollar for your thoughts," I interrupt the silence.

"A dollar?"

"Yeah, inflation." I laugh.

He chuckles and pulls me into his side. "Come on *mo Figoirhra*, time for some action!"

"What did you call me?"

"*Figoirhra* it is Gaelic for true love." He says softly, kissing me senseless.

CHAPTER 12

We hitch a ride to the top of the mountain in an old army Jeep that is painted bright green with "McCaster's Coffee Plantation on the side." There are several adventurous couples who are joining the zip-line journey. As the trucks are travelling through the forest, bumping over logs and dips and turns, I fear I'll be thrown from my seat.

I watch as each couple is rigged into a climbing harness and given instructions on how to slow and stop their progress before reaching the end of the line. Every hanging harness is attached with a carabiner clip to the pulley, which has a friction stopping mechanism that you squeeze. Heavy leather gloves and helmets are required. If you can't make the stop yourself, or something happens, there is a hand brake that is operated at the end of the line.

All three couples scream as they take off, one person at a time. When we arrive at the station, a platform built in the trees, we are instructed how to reattach our carabiner clip to another pulley on the next leg of the zip-line journey.

Now it is our turn. Robbie makes sure I am secure and

gives me a kiss as a sendoff. I did some research last night and read that some zip-lines can get up to eighty-five miles an hour on the first leg of the journey, coming down the mountain in the tree canopy. I hope it feels like flying, but I am scared.

My pulley starts out slow...but gradually I am picking up speed, however, the sound is weird and it feels like the cable isn't smooth. I start leaning to the right and I know then that something is wrong. The cable is frayed and pieces are sticking up, catching the pulley and suddenly I'm jerking to left and falling. I hit several tree branches on my way down, before I am knocked unconscious.

When I wake up, it is dark and I am still lying in the forest, but I am on top of something solid. I can tell I'm not on the ground. My body doesn't feel too bad; I can move my arms, so I slowly sit up and look around. Somewhere on the way down, I lost my helmet. My head aches on the right side and my ear has some blood caked in it. There is some blood on the back of my head, still sticky and wet in my hair.

I move one leg and it seems okay, but my left leg has pain. The nanites are busy trying to reach me. They show me where they are working by creating a picture in my thoughts of my body and put a red X where I feel the pain. I lie back down and keep quiet. I can hear voices yelling my name; Robbie sounds frantic, as his voice gets closer.

The nanites show me that my left leg is repaired, and when I move it, the pain is gone. I can live with the little bit of pain in my head. I know it will probably be healed by the time we arrive back at the hotel.

"Help!" I shout. My voice sounds shaky. I wonder when my helmet fell off.

"Opal?" Robbie shouts my name. He is right below me.

"Up on the roof!"

"Don't move!" he cautions. "I'm coming up." A few minutes later, he appears over the edge. "Where do you hurt?"

"I think I'm fine. Just rattled. I must have been knocked out." I sit up with his help.

"Is anything broken?" he asks.

"Not that I can tell. There is some sticky blood coming out of my ear and on the back of my head. I don't know what happened to the helmet."

"Aw, baby, I am so sorry!" He kisses me lightly. Let me see you rotate your lovely head. He takes out a small flashlight, as he sets the big one aside. "Look at my finger." He watches my pupils shrink. "No concussion that I can see. Let me get you off this roof. Can you stand?" His arms around me, he lifts me to my feet. "This is a miracle. I was worried you were killed. Woman, I have never been so scared in my life!"

"I think I can walk." I put pressure on my legs and take several small steps. "My legs seem to be okay."

Robbie hands me off to a man on a ladder that helps me down and is right behind me. Before I can turn, his arm circles my shoulders. I feel rather woozy and almost fall, but he scoops me up in his arms and carries me out of the woods to the waiting truck. I sit quietly next to him all the way back. The hum we share comforts me.

He gathers me up, when we return to the plantation, and carries me into a large house behind the hotel and into the kitchen, where he turns on all the lights and begins gathering hot water and first aid supplies.

"Robbie, I just need a shower or a bath." I stop him.

"Opal," he hugs me close. "God, I thought I had lost you. We have been searching the woods for hours." His eyes are watery and he kisses me urgently.

"Okay, I'll run the water. Here is a hot cup of tea with honey. Drink it down. You need the sugar."

There is knocking at the door and Robbie answers it. Stephanie comes in and hurries over to me.

"Thank God!" She exclaims. "We couldn't find you."

"I just woke up. I landed on a shed roof."

"You are bleeding." She picks up an ice pack and massages it with her hands. "Put this on your head."

"I think I'll be alright. I just need a bath. Can you go to my room and get me some sweats or something comfortable to wear?"

She shakes her head whispering. "You know you should be dead, don't you?"

"Really? The trees broke my fall and the shed roof isn't as hard as the ground."

She looks skeptical.

"I don't know when I lost the helmet."

"They are still trying to figure out what happened. The cable is frayed, but it worked fine before you got on it."

"It started sounding funny about one third of the way into the trip and then the pulley started leaning to the right, but slipped off the cable on the left. Then I was flying towards the ground." I start shivering.

"Robbie was literally unglued. He had all the people he could find combing the forest for you. He could only guess where you went down, as he was occupied getting into a hanging harness. When he looked around, there was no sign of you. He said he heard the cracking of tree limbs and that is what caused him to search the cable for you. He was like a crazy man!" Stephanie shivers.

Robbie comes back. The water is ready.

"I'll help her Robbie." Stephanie says as she slips her arm around me.

He looks on helplessly. "What can I do?"

"I think the farm manager is waiting to speak to you." Stephanie says nodding towards the door.

"Yeah, I'll go see what he has found."

He looks angry, but gives me a quick kiss before he heads out the door. When he leaves, I feel empty and alone.

She looks at me, and smiles, shaking her head. "Like I said, totally smitten."

I stay in the bath until Stephanie returns with some clothes. She also brings my shampoo, conditioner, and my backpack. I wash my hair and feel my head with my fingers. The nanites give me the all clear. I clean my ear as best I can.

I am dressed and sitting in the kitchen when Robbie comes back. He looks stressed. "Stephanie said she would order us some food and have it sent over. I'm not letting you out of my sight tonight."

"So, what happened? Could they tell what caused the fraying cable?"

He waits a while, just looking at me from a distance. Then his eyes close and he growls.

"Well then." I laugh.

"It looks like someone sabotaged the cable." He sounds totally wiped out emotionally. "It is too dark to tell. We'll be able to see better in the morning."

"It couldn't have been the sweet couples who went before us and I didn't see anybody else."

Robbie lays his head in my lap and hugs me. "How is your head?"

"Good as new. I washed out the blood and I can't even feel a scratch. I may have some bruising, but in a few short days I should be fine."

He shakes his head looking at me. His face only inches from my own. His arms wrapped around me still my quaking. I lay my head against his and I smell his hair.

I smile and lean in for a kiss. He obliges. His lips are hungry at first, but then soften. He gathers me into a hug and holds me like he needs to hold on. He breathes in the fresh scent of my damp hair and makes a trembling sigh. He kisses my cheek and stands when there is a knock at the door.

Dinner is a simple fare with soup, salad, and flan for desert. I tell Robbie I can go to my room, but he insists that he is keeping me close to make sure I won't go into shock. He carries me around like an invalid and places me in his bed. He kisses me sweetly and leaves to shower. I am asleep before he returns.

I wake up with arms around me. I stretch and turn over to face Robbie.

He smiles at me. "Sorry, but you were having bad dreams and I was only trying to comfort you."

"Uh huh." I scoot closer to him. "This is nice. Mm, you smell so good."

He kisses me and untangles himself from my embrace. The phone is ringing. He rolls over and answers it. "Got it!"

"Sorry, baby. Gotta go. The police inspector is here and needs to talk to me." He changes and heads to the door, turning just as he's about to leave. "Stay close and don't leave Stephanie's side. She can use you in the gift shop if you want to help. I have no doubt the police will want to speak with you."

I return to my room and change. My phone is dead so I don't know if Preston or Damaris has tried to call. I find the charger and plug it in.

Dressed in a sundress and sandals with my hair brushed into a braid, I go in search of a cup of coffee and some breakfast.

Robbie acted strange this morning; I guess he is worried about the investigation. It felt good to wake up in his arms. I could easily fall in love with this guy, even though we really don't know each other. Then I remember I am still married. If I fake my death, does that leave me open to remarry?

Preston will have to divorce me before I die. That way, I won't be married to him and can get remarried in another country. Divorce; I will need to add that to my list of requirements.

※ ※ ※ ※ ※

Stephanie heard from Damaris this morning. She said her nephew and sister were going to be okay. Damaris was going to stay with them until they are better. She says that

Thomas and Preston won't be back for another ten days and that I should end my reservation at the beach hotel and plan to stay at the coffee farm. Damaris will try to be back before our husbands.

I scarf down two croissants and two espressos for breakfast. Such an appetite! Stephanie puts me to work in the gift shop, handing me a walkie-talkie in case I have any questions.

The morning and afternoon fly. Robbie comes by and says that I am needed at the police station to make a statement. Stephanie is recruited as an interpreter.

They ask me to tell them exactly what happened from the moment I arrived at the beginning of the zip course, until I was found. I say it was an accident and they rant shouting in Spanish.'

"Opal," Stephanie starts. "It wasn't an accident. Someone sabotaged that cable. The police think it's either a plot to bring scandal on the farm or an attempt at murder."

I am stunned. "Murder?"

"That's the way they're looking at it," she says softly.

"I'm sure they are wrong about murder. It is probably metal fatigue or something like that."

"Fatiga del metal, no! Ácido, yes!" the policeman shouts.

Stephanie takes my hand. "They are looking for the couples who went before you. There is a missing pulley among the ones that should have been left at the end of the first leg of the journey. However, as far as they can tell, the couple gave false identification when they signed in for their appointment."

"All of them?"

"No, just the last couple," she says.

"But they were so nice and seemed very normal. She was a little nervous and he was trying to give her courage. I can't believe they had anything to do with sabotage."

"Then why give a false name?" Stephanie interprets for the policeman.

The police talk with Stephanie and she takes my hand and tells me we're leaving.

"Gracias," I say to the policeman.

Stephanie nods and we walk out.

Robbie meets the car when we arrive back at the farm. He is sporting a large sun hat and has a glass of ice water. He is filthy and in need of a shower and a clean change of clothes.

"Well," Stephanie stares at Robbie. "Guess I'll get back to the kitchen and make sure dinner plans are underway."

"Thanks for your help, Stephanie." Robbie kisses her cheek.

She smiles at him. "You know I will do anything for you."

"Nice look." I smile at him.

He doesn't smile. "Are you okay?"

"I'm sure they are wrong about that young couple. Maybe something in the pulley released the acid." I search his face.

"Then why use aliases?" He says seriously. "I'm thinking I should get you away from here."

"They weren't after me, Robbie. Who would want me dead?"

My voice lowers as my mind returns to my conversation with Preston. No. Preston wouldn't go to that trouble to get me out of his life. I won't believe it!

Robbie puts his arm around me and leads me to the house, then pours me a glass of cola and tells me to drink it down. "The sugar helps with shock." He advises me.

I just stare at him. My emotions are numb. "Why did this happen to me?" I whisper.

His kisses along my neck make me shiver with anticipation while I wait for his lips to touch mine. I turn my lips to meet his and run my hands up his chest laying them on his muscular pecks and over his heart. I can feel his heart racing. He murmurs deep in his throat, then slowly brakes away.

"Did that help?" He smiles slyly.

"Yep, I am still alive and kicking." I release a noisy puff of air and smile back at him.

"Now, about that relationship you are trying to get over. Is it something we should be concerned about?"

He surprises me with this question. I don't know what to say. Yes, Preston wants me to play dead. He had actually said his life and our family's lives will be better if I died, but I can't believe he would resort to murder to remove me from his life. Besides, we were on pretty good terms when he left. He even gave me a goodbye kiss and laughed at my antics. How would he have known I was going to take the zip-line tour? He doesn't even know I am at the coffee farm. As far as he is concerned, I'm still at the beach.

"No," I am resolved where Preston is concerned. He isn't involved in this attempt at sabotaging the zip cable. "The person I am involved with doesn't even know I am here at the farm. He thinks I'm still at the beach. I'm sure of it."

"Okay," Robbie said. "Then we have to check out other scenarios."

"I don't believe it was anyone after me, Robbie. We didn't make a reservation for the tour and the only ones who knew what we planned to do are you, Stephanie, and me."

Stephanie is in touch with Dr. Rushing. Maybe someone there had gotten hold of the information. That is something I can't discuss with Robbie, but I can talk to Stephanie and find out whom she might have told.

"I need to talk to Stephanie," I say, walking away.

"Wait, I'll go with you."

"I'm sorry, but this is between her and me." I open the door, but turn to see I had hurt him. "Hey, I'll come back and tell you later." I blow him a kiss, but he doesn't respond.

Stephanie is in the dining room when I find her. "I need to speak with you." I say quietly. "Alone."

"What's up?" She put down the stack of silverware she is carrying.

"Did you tell Dr. Rushing that I am here?"

"No," she says knitting her brows. "Why?"

"Robbie thinks someone is trying to kill me."

"Well, let's see," she starts. "Who wants you dead?"

"Preston doesn't even know I'm here. He still thinks I'm at the beach. We were on pretty good terms when he left, he even kissed me goodbye."

"He kissed you?" she asks.

"On the forehead." I explain. "And he was joking, so I don't think it was him."

"Why would Dr. Rushing want to hurt you?"

"Maybe she is just trying to scare me." I say.

"But how would she know you were going to go to the zip-line?"

"That is why I asked you if you talked with her. She could send in spies. She is ruthless when it comes to what she wants. It doesn't matter what we go through as long as she gets what she deems is necessary to her project."

I pace the room.

"She doesn't know you are here. I promise." Stephanie says.

"Then the sabotage wasn't meant for me. It must have been done to hurt the farm; competition from another plantation?"

"Hmmm." Stephanie looks thoughtful. "I need to speak with Robbie, alone."

"Whatever, I'm going to my room to take a hot shower and change. Can you please have someone send a tray to my room? I don't care what you choose. I'm not very hungry."

"Robbie isn't going to agree with that," she says. "He doesn't want you out of his sight."

"He'll just have to get over it!" I turn on my heel and leave in a huff, hearing Robbie ask Stephanie where I was going.

CHAPTER 13

Back in my room, I get into the shower. The hot water feels like it should wash all this weirdness away. I soap up a couple of times, but can't wash my hair since my shampoo is at Robbie's. I rinse it really well and then sit in the bottom of the tub and let the water continue until it turns cold.

Someone is knocking on the door. I wrap my robe around me and answer it.

"Who's there?"

"It's me, sweetness. Can I come in?" Robbie asks.

I open the door and throw myself in his arms. He seems satisfied to wrap his arms around me and bury his head in my neck. I have to admit I feel very safe in his capable arms.

He growls. "I can't take any more of this. We have to get you to a safe place."

"Robbie, this isn't about me. Darling I promise it isn't." I try to persuade him.

"Opal," he sighs, "Do you know what I went through when I saw that you weren't anywhere around and I heard the tree limbs breaking? I was so damn scared you had been killed, I couldn't think straight.

"Shhhh." I croon "It is over and I am right here in your arms. Don't think about that anymore. I'll get dressed and we can go back to your place." I pull clothes out of my suitcase and step into the bathroom to dress.

I check my phone and unplug the charger. No messages.

We stop in to tell Stephanie to have enough food for two sent to Robbie's. She smiles a knowing smile that says, "See I told you he wouldn't let you stay by yourself."

After dinner, we sit on the couch and contemplate our next move, staring into each other's eyes contentedly. Finally, I make the first move and straddle his lap. We sit that way for some time, until I start unbuttoning his shirt and kissing my way down his rock hard chest. He only lets me unbutton two before he takes my head in his hands and lifts my face to his lips. His tongue slips easily into my mouth seeking mine. I finish unbuttoning his shirt and run my hands over his chest. His hand slips up my shirt and rubs my ribs, making its way up to my breast. He cups my breast and moans. His fingers make small circles on my nipple and I whimper. He brakes free from my mouth and looks at me.

"Make love to me," I whisper.

He picks me up, my legs wrapping around him and in no time we are in his room. He pulls my shirt over my head and pulls his off as well. His mouth finds mine again and then makes its way down my neck to my collarbone, placing feather like kisses along the way. My body trembles as his breath cools my skin and his hands cup my breasts.

"God, you are beautiful!" He growls and takes my nipple in his mouth, making round circles with his tongue and causing every nerve in my body to quake with delight.

I reach down to unhook his belt and unzip his shorts, pushing them down over his hips. He goes commando. I stroke him and he groans with pleasure and quickly strips off my panties. His eyes take in the blonde curls and he grins.

He lays me on the bed and begins stroking my body with his hands. His fingers slip between my folds and find my hard nub. "So wet. So ready for me," he sighs.

I take a long breath and then softly whisper, "I'm a virgin."

He freezes instantly and looks up at my face.

I smile. He smiles back and slips his hand between my legs. As he leans across me to the nightstand to grab a foil packet, I lick and nip at his nipple as it drags across my mouth.

"Baby, the night will end right here and now if you keep that up."

I watch as he rolls the condom down his very large shaft. I take it in my hand to measure its width. "Will it fit?"

"Eventually," he says, grinning.

The small hum we usually feel when we are together gathers into a crescendo of pulsating resonance at our joining. "Oh my God, what was that? Did you feel that?"

"I still do. I told you we were meant to be together." He kisses my neck and reaches down to pinch my nipples. "Let's do that again!"

We make love all night long and finally fall into an exhausted sleep.

I wake up content when I realize Robbie's arms are still around me. I watch his face for some time. His long dark eyelashes lay on his cheeks and he looks younger when he's sleeping; more like a twenty five-year-old. His body is perfect, a wonderful specimen. His lashes start moving and he suddenly opens his eyes and looks into mine.

"Good morning, sweetness." He kisses my palm. "I didn't hurt you did I?"

"It hurt a little bit, but other sensations took over." I rub his belly admiring the way his hair grows on his chest and makes a line to his manhood.

"Ready for a repeat performance?" He asks.

I lean in and kiss him, sucking on his bottom lip and stroking him. He pushes me onto my back and pleasures me before he tries to enter me. He tries and tries, but he can't get in.

"What is wrong?" He asks confused.

Oh shit! The nanites have repaired my hymen, but they've made it impenetrable. I quickly jump up from the bed and run to the bathroom. "Be right back." I call to him. I calm down and try to contact the nanites. I imagine sex, showing them that once the hymen is broken it has to stay that way. I wait a while and then they show me it is gone.

"Sorry," I say when I return to the bedroom. "Now where were we?"

"What was that?" He asks.

I gently grab him and stroke. He shuts up, pushing me onto my back and making passionate love to me twice before we decide we aren't going to get out of bed all day.

He makes a few phone calls and I make coffee. After a couple of cups each, we decide to shower. We wash each other's hair and like the feel of our bodies rubbing against each other while they are soapy, so we have sex in the shower. We just can't get enough of each other. It seems we can't satisfy our need to be close.

We spend the rest of the day talking about the farm and getting to know one another. Wrapped around Robbie all day is like a dream come true. Lying in bed after a round of lovemaking, we curl up in each other's arms, falling asleep from sheer exhaustion. We sleep until morning. That hum is so comforting, and it is an integral part of our coupling.

I wake up with him raining kisses all over my neck and

back, while his hand moves in between my legs, finding all the places that give me pleasure, his other caresses by breasts.

When we are both fully satisfied, we gaze into each other's eyes. If the eyes are the window to the soul, then his soul is the most beautiful thing I have ever seen. No ifs, ands, buts, or maybes; I am falling in love.

"I love you, Opal," Robbie confesses. He kisses me tenderly, his lips gently moving against mine. "I know it seems too soon to say this, but I know what I feel for you. I don't ever want to be without you."

"I love you, Robbie. I actually understand what you mean. It does seem too soon, but I know…just know that there are opportunities that one can't pass up." I caress his face.

"Marry me." He says surprising me. "Today. Marry me."

"I can't marry you today," I sigh. The time I am dreading had finally come. I worry about what he will think. Will he order me out of his house? He might think I am a freak and bolt.

"I'm already married. I've been married to the same man for thirty-five years."

He laughs. "You're not even thirty-five years old."

"No, I'm fifty-six years old."

The smile falls from his face. "You're serious?"

"Yes."

"B…But how?" he stammers.

"There is a clinic in Switzerland where I went for a skin procedure, but because of some misdirected nanites, they recreated my entire body." I continue. He needs to know it all.

"I was having problems in my marriage. My husband doesn't find me desirable anymore so I thought if I looked younger he would want me again. Not true. He told me that I had been away too long, the procedure took about three months, and that he has found someone else. The someone else, turned out to be my best friend. My husband and I met here in Guatemala to talk things over. He still wants to declare me dead, saying that it will be too hard for my family to accept who I am now."

"So he wants you dead? That's harsh. Especially since you have been married so many years." He jumps off the bed. "What am I saying? I'm totally freaked-out here! Please tell me this is all a joke," he pleads.

"Sorry. It's not a joke. If it is, it's on me. The doctor calls it a do-over. I've lost my home and my family. I don't care about the husband. He is an entirely selfish human being. But I miss my daughter and grandchild."

"This is the guy you are trying to get over?"

"Believe me, someone wanting you to pretend you're dead helps with that." I walk into the bathroom and brush my teeth.

"Wow!"

"Still love me?" I laugh. "I didn't want this to go any further until you knew, so you can change your mind. I wasn't sure you weren't just playing a game to get into my panties, until I saw how you responded when I was hurt. Then, I realized you were serious." I start shaking. "I'm sorry. I feel like I've lead you on, but just so you know, my feelings are real."

"So you don't think your husband did this?"

"No, he doesn't even know I left the beach."

"Does he want you back?" He asks a little miffed.

"No. He wants to declare me dead, remember? I told him he can, if he introduces me to the family as my niece. My brother died several years back and my daughter has never met her. Well, they couldn't meet her since she doesn't exist. But it is the only way I know to be with my daughter and granddaughter."

"Too confusing!" He scratches his head.

"Now I want Preston to divorce me before I'm supposed to be dead."

"Why are you agreeing to this? Just go back and make everyone deal with the new you."

"There is also the problem with the clinic. They really don't want the fact that I exist to get out. It would create too much chaos. I'm already someone's science project; I don't want to end up some government's project, too."

"You are never going to age?" He looks skeptical.

"Well, never is a long time. The nanites fix everything that is wrong. I was really hurt on that roof. My left leg was broken and my right arm was hurt. My head was banged up pretty bad and I had blood coming out of my ear. Most of it was repaired before I woke up. And the reason you couldn't get in yesterday was because they fixed my hymen and made it stronger."

His mouth is open in shock.

"Robbie, breathe." I smile.

He exhales with a whistle. "So you what? You ran in the bathroom and broke it yourself? You mean you could stay a virgin?"

"No I can communicate with them and teach them what's supposed to happen. I told them sex was natural and that the hymen didn't need to be repaired."

I take off my robe and throw it on the bed, reaching for my clothes to get dressed. I search for my sandals.

"Where are you going?"

"Back to my room." Tears formed in my eyes as I brace myself for rejection.

"I can't say I'm not shocked and a little disturbed, but I don't want you to leave. We still don't know what is going on and I'm not going to take the chance of something happening to you." His arm reaches out and pulls me to him. "I don't care who you were. I love who you are." He kisses me with the same fervency as before.

I stare into the face of this gorgeous man who claims to love me and is still protecting me. Most of my life I've dreamed of a love like Robbie has shown me the past couple of days. The pressure in my chest at the thought of losing him is suffocating me.

"Opal, breathe." He smiles as he cups my cheek and leans in to kiss it.

"Um...do you think you could put on some clothes? You are driving me crazy!"

He laughs and goes to his closet to get dressed.

"So who else knows about this? Stephanie?"

"Yeah, she knows. I can't tell you how she found out. That is her story." I find my sandals under the couch.

He stands behind me with his brush. "I wanted to do this yesterday and didn't. May I?" he asks. I turn to look at him. He has so much love and acceptance in his eyes. Turning around, I sit in the kitchen chair. He draws the brush in long tender strokes down my hair. When he gets to a part that is tangled, he gently pulls it apart. He brushes my hair for thirty minutes. It feels cathartic, soul cleansing, like a good foot washing ceremony at church. When he is finished, he pulls the hair out of his brush and looks at them in the sunlight shining through the kitchen window.

"Spun gold." He smiles. "I knew you were an angel." He pulls me into his arms and kisses me with such sweetness I think I will melt.

"So, you still love me?" I don't look at him.

"Hey," he turns my face to his, "I like older women. They make better lovers."

CHAPTER 14

We work on the farm during the day and make love every night. There are no more "accidents." I like our routine and the days fly by; until I finally get the call I have been dreading. Preston is back in Antiqua. He is waiting for me to meet him at the hotel. I hate to leave Robbie and the farm, but he understands that this has to be.

The police never found the perpetrators of the zip-line fiasco and there aren't any more leads. The missing pulley is still unaccounted for, so the investigation is put on hold.

Robbie drives me to the hotel and says he will wait for me. I tell him to go back to the farm and I will call him. He is reluctant to leave me, but I insist that this conversation has to take place. He says he wants to wait nearby.

I walk into the hotel lobby and Preston steps up to take my bag. He looks older and a bit haggard. "We are this way," he indicates by taking the lead and walking down the hall.

"Are you alright?" I ask. "You don't look so good."

He sighs. "I'm not so good, Opal, just a bit under the weather. The meetings went well, but dealing with overseas banks can be hell. I'll be fine in a few days. I'm not a spring chicken, you know?"

"Of course. Um....are we staying together in this room? There is only one bed."

"I don't know, I thought we could give our relationship a chance. Isn't that what you want?" He smirks pulling me into his arms.

"What the hell!" I push him away. "You have a girlfriend remember?"

"She doesn't have to know."

"You disgust me!"

"I still love you," he says. "I was just put off by the new appearance."

"Well, thank you very much for your change of heart, but I am going to tell you exactly what you are going to do. You are going to divorce me. Then you are going to declare me dead and hold a funeral. There won't be any need for a body. Just tell everyone I am an organ donor."

"Why do I have to divorce you?"

"Because I have fallen in love with someone else and want to marry him." I say sincerely.

"How could you fall in love so quickly? You wanted me back just a few weeks ago." He is skeptical.

"I fell out of love with you the moment you told me about Tess." I don't spare his feelings.

"Who is he?"

"His name is Robbie Brand. I met him several weeks ago. We love each other."

"Robbie Brand? Robbie Brand...." He knitted his brows. "Where have I heard that name before? He is that lead singer in that *Inventing Abbey* band isn't he? Surely you don't mean that guy?"

"That is exactly who I mean. How would you know about him? You don't listen to that kind of music do you?" I ask.

"Sure, when I started hanging out with Tess; she listens to that stuff." He smiles. "She had a magazine with an article about the band members. He has never been married before. Said he hadn't found the right girl. You know, some people speculate he just hasn't come out of the closet yet."

I laugh. "Believe me, he isn't gay!"

"So you slept with him?"

"Yeah, Dad, what of it? How dare you ask me about my sex life? Haven't you been banging my best friend?"

My phone rings; it's Robbie so I answer it. "Hey," I speak into the phone. "I'm fine. Come on up. We are in room 119."

"Who is it?"

I answer the door. Robbie steps into the room and faces Preston. I move between them and Robbie walks over to me, drawing me close and kissing me passionately.

"Sorry," he says, "but I didn't want him to get any ideas."

I smile at him. "I already told him. Now, do you want to take a seat while we finish talking? There are some complications."

"Like what?" Robbie draws up a chair to be closer.

I look at Preston. He isn't very receptive to the new person in the room. "Preston has decided he wants to sleep with me; never mind he has a girlfriend."

"That is our business." Preston says.

"No Preston," I correct him. "I love Robbie and if he still wants me, I am going to marry him. It is also his business, since you have asked me to take up my wifely duties."

"I thought he has another woman and wants to tell everyone you are dead?" He scowls at Preston.

"He is going to give me a divorce before I marry you. Then after a few weeks he will tell everyone that I didn't make it."

"You are going on tour in a few months. We will try to get together as much as possible. If you don't want to tie yourself down to me before your tour, I will understand. We can wait until the tour is over."

He was out of the chair in an instant, taking me in his arms. "Oh sweetness, the sooner we are husband and wife the better. I don't want to wait."

Preston stood up. "Please, can you stop? You are making me sick. All this lovey-dovey mess is something I don't need to see!" He turns to me. "Besides, you are still my wife."

"In name only! I haven't been your wife in years." I huff. Robbie pushes me into the hall and shuts the door. He's gotten a room on the second floor for us. After several hours of lovemaking, Robbie and I settle down to a discussion. He understands my need to make sure my daughter is safe from the manipulations of her father.

"I told you that I love you and I will wait until your divorce is final, but I won't wait until the tour is over. I can't stand the thought of you being married to that guy. He is a ruthless, thoughtless, selfish, self-centered, egotistical bastard."

I chuckle. "Yep, he is that."

Preston leaves the next day. He needs time to arrange a quickie divorce, so we head back to the farm. He says he'll be in touch and send the divorce papers. I tell him that it has to remain a secret; I don't want Laura to know he's divorcing me. I also tell him that I expect him to include Leslie Garmond in his will.

Back at the farm, we continue where we left off. I find out Robbie is the real owner of the farm and that he purchased it to help Stephanie and Garrett, since they didn't have the means to get it up and running when they bought it. They have been friends for years and Stephanie is like family to him.

Robbie tells me about his parents and how they had burned to death along with his baby sister, in a house fire in Scotland. He lived with relatives until he turned twenty-one, then he moved out and started his band.

Most of the band members are childhood friends of his, but to me they all appear much older than Robbie. He says it is because they live harder, drink too much, do drugs, and have lots of loose women. He says the lifestyle ages them.

His fascination with eating healthier and having his own organic garden help him stay young. He also doesn't eat red meat or chicken. I see him eat fish, so I guess you can call him a pescetarian. I find myself falling deeper in love with him every day. I have never met such a tenderhearted man.

About three weeks after Preston left for home, I receive a package with the divorce papers. I take them to a lawyer Stephanie trusts and he makes a few suggestions and then I sign them and send them back. Three weeks after that, I am a divorced woman with $250,000 in my account.

Robbie surprises me with a small wedding in the flower garden on the coffee farm. I am now Mrs. McCaster, Robbie's real name; Brand being his stage name. We take off a week later and honeymoon in Tahiti for a week and then travel to Italy where we rent a house in Tuscany for a month.

When we return to Guatemala, there is a letter from Preston telling me Laura is gravely ill. He says the doctors think it is Leukemia. Robbie's European Tour starts in Germany in two weeks. I planned on going with him, but now I will return to Nashville to begin the lie. The only good thing is seeing my family again. I can't wait to see Lucy. It has been almost six months. She is now five. Laura needs her mom, but Cousin Leslie will be the one returning. I'll even be there for my own memorial.

We make the next week the best, never leaving each other's side for longer than an hour or two. Love doesn't happen like this to everyone, but I am happy that I have met Robbie. He makes plans to visit Nashville in the spring. We promise to text and phone every day. I cry when I know he isn't looking.

It is going to be Thanksgiving when I meet my family as twenty-five year old Leslie Garmond. Preston has set up the apartment just as I have specified. He has told Laura that Leslie is coming to Nashville to live and will be taking care of her and Lucy.

The night before I am to leave, Robbie and I hold each other all night long, whispering sentiments of love. "I love you, Opal." He squeezes me close. "How I am going to do this. Baby? I need you to know that I don't want this separation. I understand why you need to go, but I don't like it."

"Robbie, I love you, too, but I have to do this for my daughter and granddaughter. I have to be there for Laura. Preston won't be; he has finally retired and he and Tess were married last week. They are taking off for an extended stay in Florida. You're coming to visit in February, that's just a few months."

"Then I'll have the torture of leaving you all over again." He moans.

"Let's not think of that; only of being together and loving one another. I can't wait for you to meet my Laura and Lucy."

He smiles. "Lucy is the only one you ever mention."

"Yeah, I'm kind of crazy about her, like I am about you. Maybe one day we can have a child." I have been daydreaming of having Robbie's child; maybe a little girl with his black hair and blue eyes or a little boy with his beautiful lips and dimples. We aren't doing anything to prevent a child, so it is possible.

"I have never heard of anyone with MEMs having children, but nothing is impossible. Usually the MEMs look on the pregnancy as a burden and destroy the fetus. Maybe if I communicate my desire they will leave it alone."

"There is time for one last round of love making. Are you game?" I kiss his chest.

Our passion moves with a ferocity we haven't

experienced before and touched with a bit of sadness. We are consumed with having as much of each other as we can get, but exhaustion finally claims us as we fall asleep in each other's arms.

Baggage loaded and time for our last goodbye, we cry and hold each other.

"Baby, I'm not ready to say goodbye," Robbie stares long and hard into my eyes. "How will I be able to keep you safe so far from me?"

"I'll keep me safe and you'll keep you safe, because I won't be able to live without you, Robbie. I'm already looking forward to your visit in February. Where will you be during Christmas?"

He sighs leaning his forehead against mine. "I'll try to get away and find you."

The loud speaker rings with the last call for my flight. Robbie pulls me in and holds me tight. "I love you, Opal, my darling wife."

CHAPTER 15

Preston meets me at the airport. He seems chipper and anxious. Tess is with her family in New York. She will meet Preston for their honeymoon next week.

"Leslie," he says grinning. "Welcome to Nashville. You had a pleasant flight, I hope." He motions towards Laura. Now I know why he is acting strange. I reach out to shake Laura's hand.

"You must be Laura. Pleasure to meet you." I drop to my knees. "And you must be Lucy. Aren't you a pretty thing?" I can't help myself and draw her into a tight hug.

"Nice to meet you, Leslie. Dad has been filling me in on your wish to meet us. We are glad to have you for Thanksgiving. He says you have an apartment here in town, so we'll drop your bags by there before we head back home for Thanksgiving dinner."

"I have been alone for some time, so getting to know my family is important for me."

I am stunned at Laura's appearance. She is thinner than I have ever seen her with dark circles under her eyes. "You look a lot like my mom must have looked when she was younger." She confesses. "Quite unnerving, really."

"I wish I could have met her." I smile.

Preston takes my things to my apartment. He isn't able to take his eyes off me. Maybe he regrets the way he's treated me, but I think it is old-fashioned lust.

The dinner at Laura's is comfortable, but it's hard for me to keep my emotions under control. Just seeing Laura and Lucy make me want to confess who I am and give them a hug. Preston comes to my aid.

"Lucy, can you tell Leslie how many languages you can count to ten?"

She stares at me. "Do I know you?"

I pick her up. "My name is Leslie and I am a relative of yours. Do you know what a relative is?"

"It means we are related." She answers.

I hug her. "Right! We have the same eye color and maybe you can find other things that both of us share, that show we are related."

Laura joined our conversation. "You look a lot like my mom. I can see her in many ways; like her smile or her small ears." She has tears in her eyes. "I am pleased to have you here, Leslie. Mom's memorial will be on Saturday. I really didn't want to have it on a holiday. Then the holiday is always filled with painful memories."

I hold out my arm to her and she joins Lucy and me in a hug. "I'm so sorry about Aunt Opal. I did hope to meet her when I moved here," I say.

We all play with the Wii and laugh with all Lucy's antics. Of course the picture albums are brought out and I sit holding back tears the rest of the time. We really are lucky. Our lives were filled with love and happiness for each other, during the years that Laura was growing up.

Preston and I leave around 7:00 p.m. and he drives me to my apartment. He says he has purchased a small car for me, handing me the keys. I find it parked in the garage as he said.

My apartment is one-half of a converted house. It seems that everything I had asked for is in the apartment, including a stocked fridge. There are a few things I want to purchase, like new curtains and paint. The counter top needs replacing and I want to get rid of the carpeting and put in hardwood floors. Preston clears his throat, interrupting my thoughts. I didn't know he had followed me.

"Well, that seemed to go pretty well. I thought you were going to lose it there when you picked up Lucy."

I look at him. "Yes, thanks for the save."

"We can always tell them the truth." He says sadly.

"So how are you really doing? Glad Tess isn't here. That would have been awkward."

"I never told her, you know. She believes you're dead. I

didn't want to advertise what happened to you to anyone." He shakes his head. "Not because I'm embarrassed, but because it's your private life. I wanted to make it easier on you."

Well shit. Here I was already to whip her ass for having an affair with my husband.

"Press, I'm sorry things didn't work out for us."

He raises my hand and kisses it. "My mistake." I hear the front door close behind him.

My first night without Robbie is horrible and I am crying when my phone rings.

"Didn't think you would get away from me that easy did you?" he says. "Where is your apartment?"

"Are you in the States?" I say hopefully.

"No, baby, I wish. I just want to look up your location on Google. So I can feel like I know where you are."

I tell him about dinner with the family, my apartment, and my new car. Robbie tells me that the band is excited about the new tour, but he is lonely in the middle of the maelstrom that is the life of a celebrity. He promises me this is his last tour.

We sit for a long time, neither one of us speaking, trying to fathom how we came to this separation, wanting it to end. We finally say our "I love yous" and tearful "goodbyes."

His last words are, "I miss our hum."

I fall asleep dreaming of his arms around me and wake

full of hope that he is in my bed for real. I have faith that Robbie and I will survive any storm thrown at us. We are connected on a much deeper level than just emotions or physical needs. This hum we are aware of, binds us on all levels. He has become a part of me. When we are together, there is an immutable link that connects us to one another. It's as if my blood calls to his when we are apart.

The car waiting in the garage is a small hatchback Subaru. It is also full of gas, so I take it out to do some shopping. On my way home, I stop by my old home to find Preston in an ugly mood.

"Why didn't you call me back? Did you even get my message?"

I smile at his ranting. "Yes, Uncle Press," I say, "I did get your message, but there are things I needed to take care of before I came over this morning."

He huffs. "What?"

"Black Friday, biggest shopping day of the year!" I say. "What do you need?"

"Well, I thought we could go over the job description, so that there will be no confusion as to what I expect." He sat down at the kitchen table with a list.

"What the hell do you mean by job description? This isn't a freaking job! I'm here to help my daughter and granddaughter. I don't work for you!"

"I just set you up with an apartment and I bought you a car. You need to be aware that you need to fulfill some requirements."

"Ha! What do you want me to do wash dishes, do laundry?"

"Well, actually, Tess and I talked about it and…"

"Tess has no say whatsoever in my life. We are divorced, so you don't have any control over what I do. As a matter of fact, you got off fairly cheap with our divorce. I know how much is in your 401K and IRAs, so just be glad I settled on the small amount I did." I spin on my heel and walk towards the door. "Consider it silence money. Oh, and before I forget, I need some more money."

"What for?"

"I need to fix up the apartment. Paint, new counter tops. I ordered a new bed for the bedroom and want a table and chairs."

"Oh," he hands me his platinum credit card. "Get whatever you need. You'll probably need some new clothes for the winter."

He reaches for me and I let him hug me.

"I'm sorry," he says. "I really didn't think things through when I let you get away from me."

✌ ✌ ✌ ✌ ✌

There are many people at my memorial service. Laura

and Preston have done splendidly with all the arrangements. My favorite church hymns are played, as well as the two songs I wrote, that are being sung by a friend of Laura's. She has a picture collage set up and people walk by to pay their last respects and reminisce about their memories.

I spend a great deal of time just looking at the experiences life brought my way. I had a good life. I know Laura is remembering her childhood. She has always been a well-adjusted, happy person. She blows a kiss heavenward. "Thanks Mom. You were my best friend and hero."

Next day, I stop at Preston's and tell he can go with me to help order the counter tops and choose paint. It seems to make him happier.

I spend the next week helping Laura, by watching Lucy. We play together in the park and watch the Christmas Spectacular production of The Nutcracker in Nashville. She can't keep her eyes open for the entire event so I pick her up and hold her through the last half.

Christmas will be here soon and I wonder how Robbie's plans for making it to Nashville are going. He said it didn't seem likely he could get away, but that he isn't through giving up hope. I tell him I will try to get to him if he can't get to me. He is in Moscow and says I won't be able to travel without a visa and a travel permit and that it will take me too long to wait for those papers.

The apartment is coming along nicely. All the extra furniture I bought has arrived and I spend several days painting and hanging drapes. I buy a small tree and decorate it. My present to Robbie is a picture from our wedding. The artist has taken the liberty to use his imagination and it captures our countenances; totally enraptured.

🕊🕊🕊🕊🕊

I am at a coffee shop across the street when I feel the current run through me. I know he is somewhere around. I am searching the sidewalks, consumed with finding him.

"Hello sweetness." He is smiling at me As I dive into his embrace. Our mouths lock in a hungry kiss that takes my breath away. I look up at him and a needful cry escapes my mouth. He kisses me softly.

"I missed you!" I say tears running down my face.

"Me too," he says, his eyes are also full of unshed tears. "Come, let's get off the street." He looks around, hiding his face in my neck.

I plop my baseball cap on his head. "Oh, I forgot. You are a celebrity over here." I take his hand and lead him across the street to my apartment.

I look up the street towards the crosswalk and think I see Zoe standing in the crowd. She has an angry look on her face. It is only my imagination I convince myself. What would she be doing here? When I look up again, she is gone.

We enter the apartment and start taking off our clothes before we get to the bedroom. His hands slip under my sweater and gently rub my breasts, circling my nipples, making me moan with delight. His head comes down and his mouth captures mine in a deep kiss. We finish undressing and then we are under the covers making up for lost time.

"Opal," he whispers. "I have missed this. You are such a part of me."

My phone rings and I ignore it. I don't care who wants to speak to me. Only Robbie matters. We lie in each other's arms and hold on like we need the other for a life-line. We make love again and sleep until late in the morning.

I finally check my messages and return Laura's call. She wants to make sure I will be at her house Christmas morning to watch Lucy open her presents. I tell her my husband has surprised me and that I will be bringing him. She sounds curious, but agrees.

Robbie and I walk around the park and pick up a few more presents for Laura and Lucy.

It's Christmas Eve and I make omelets and salad for the evening meal.

"Come open your gift," I coax.

He smiles excitedly. "I love opening presents! This big one is mine?"

Robbie opens the picture and his eyes turn to me

questioning. "How did you do this? Look at our faces. This is amazing, baby, like the artist was able to capture how we feel about each other."

I stare into his eyes, which are so full of love that I feel that jolt of emotion deep inside. He didn't have to say anything. We are connected on such a deep level that I don't think there is any way we can ever be apart for long. He is leaving in a week's time for Norway and I am going with him. I can't deny my need to be near him anymore.

He hands me a small red box. Inside I find a Celtic knot ring made out of platinum, with beautiful rubies in the center of each knot. Inside the band is an inscription. "I love the way we hum R.M." We never exchanged wedding rings, so I am very happy to receive the ring that he designed especially for me.

When I look on his hand, I see that he has a similar ring without the rubies for himself. He says he wants everyone to know he is married.

"The band understands that I am happily married, although they won't believe it until they meet you." He laughs. "I told them I am married to an angel. Oh, and I forgot to tell you that I wrote three new songs after you left."

He kisses me again and we stop talking and just revel in the kisses. "You are getting better about breathing," he smiles.

"Now," I say pulling my knees to my chin. "Tell me

about the songs."

He gets up, goes to the piano, and plays one of them for me. The music and lyrics bring tears to my eyes, as he describes how our love feels and how we can survive in spite of the darkness that descends, with troubles not our own. The chorus was hauntingly beautiful.

After a brief walk around the square, we go to bed early and sleep soundly curled up in each other's arms until the alarm wake us on Christmas Morning.

We pack the car with presents and I drive to Laura's house. Preston and Tess are already there when we arrive.

Laura stares in awe when I introduce Robbie. She knows who he is and asks why my name is different. I told her it is really McCaster, that Brand was Robbie's stage name and that I use Garmond, so they wouldn't be confused about who I am when they met me. Tess is all over Robbie, so he purposely follows me to the kitchen and I try to keep him busy.

As the day progresses, I notice Preston glaring at Robbie. I decide that now is a good time to announce that I am leaving with Robbie in a week and will return in a few months.

I am surprised when Preston speaks up. "You are not going anywhere! Laura needs you." He is angry.

"I'm sorry, but you have a wife and you aren't returning to Florida until February, so I am going to go on tour with *Inventing Abbey*. Laura's doctor says she is in remission after the last trial drug." I turn to Laura. "I will check in often, to see how you are doing."

I lean in and give Robbie a kiss. His face is glowing with the revelation that we won't have to be apart.

Laura encourages me to join the band on tour. "I'm fine and I wouldn't want to be away from my husband either if it was me." She is blushing. I think my husband has a secret admirer.

"What a gorgeous ring," Tess turns my hand to get a better look.

"It is a present from Robbie for Christmas. We didn't really exchange rings when we were married and he designed it. He's a Scotsman, so he chose our wedding rings to reflect his heritage."

༄ ༄ ༄ ༄ ༄

Robbie notices something is wrong when we return to the apartment; the door isn't completely shut and the lock has been jimmied. But we are really shocked to find that someone has destroyed the Christmas tree and used a knife on the wedding picture. They have sliced down between the two of us and wrote in what looks like blood "you will regret this." There is also the scent of a cloying perfume that is not unfamiliar. "I know that smell."

Robbie wants to call the police, but I say it is probably a crazy fan and that we will be leaving soon. He insists on calling them and after several hours of pictures, fingerprints, and a trip to the station, we are permitted to return to the apartment; however, we stay at a hotel for the night at the urging of the police.

The next day, I pack my bags and ready the apartment, removing the Christmas tree and packing away the bulbs that hadn't been broken. We also run by the artist's house with the damaged painting and ask him to repaint it and mail it to Guatemala. He is surprised with the attack and the damage.

I take whatever food is left in the fridge to Preston. He promises to have an alarm installed on the apartment. He is not happy with my decision to leave. "I will be back to check on Laura as soon as I am able." I promise.

"Don't worry," he huffed. "I can take care of her."

"You would think so," I laugh.

He shakes it off. "Just go. I'm sure your husband is anxious to get out of here."

"Jealous?" I chuckle. "Well, who knew you could be jealous." I kiss his forehead. "Be good! Tess." I nod at her with a grin on my face. It feels good to know I still hold a place in Preston's heart that Tess hasn't captured.

"You be good," he shoots back.

I couldn't resist being playful. "My husband doesn't like it when I am good. He likes it when I'm very, very bad!" I laugh.

He harrumphed.

I'm not sure what Tess makes of the relationship Preston has with Leslie, but I am giddy that she doesn't own him. Part of him will always belong to Opal. After thirty-five years in a relationship with someone, it is difficult to erase all feelings. I have moved Preston into a different section of my heart.

CHAPTER 16

The concert in Norway is cancelled, due to inclement weather, so we meet the rest of the band members in Quebec, Canada. They are surprised. I'm not what they expected and let me know they thought Robbie would choose an older woman. Robbie winks at me.

The band manager has put the entire band in a suite of rooms, but Robbie and I stay in our own room on a different floor of the hotel. It seems strange to hang around a bunch of rowdy men all day; therefore I take the opportunity to do some shopping for warmer clothes. I still have Preston's credit card, so I get a "Thinking of You" card and mail it back to him.

When I return to the hotel, there is a note and a ticket from Robbie telling me to take a taxi to the Civic Center and watch the concert. He also provides a small flashlight and says I would know when to use it. I am curious.

I dress in a new pair of black skinny jeans and a willowy blouse in shades of blue to match my eyes. I take scissors to my waist length hair and cut it to the middle of my back. I wear ankle length cowboy boots with studs and check my long coat when I arrive.

The ticket is for a seat close to the stage, but not so near that I can't see the band. The sound is very loud and another singer is warming up the audience with a few ballads I have heard before. Unfortunately, I'm not up on the new sounds.

When it is time for *Inventing Abbey* to make their appearance, the audience is yelling and screaming in anticipation. Robbie walks out to the piano and plays the opening notes to the new song he had sung to me just a few days ago in my apartment. The rest of the band follows and picks up the tune on their instruments and Robbie comes to the front with his microphone.

"I'm going to start this concert off with an announcement." There is speculation running rampant that he is going to reveal that the band is breaking up.

"If you will all remain quiet." It takes several minutes for the noise to drop to a minor rumble. Robbie continues. "There is someone very special here tonight. Now if she will reveal herself, I would like to introduce her." He motions for the lights to be turned down on stage.

I know he was waiting for me to use the flashlight, so I turn it on and point it under my chin so he can see my face. "The light is a purple color and he finds me immediately.

"Come love." He holds out his hand.

I feel the hum when I get closer and the feeling of coming home envelopes me. A beefy looking guy lifts me by my waist and thrusts me up to Robbie who takes my hands and pulls me on stage. The lights brighten and he wraps me into his warm arms and gives me a big passionate kiss before he speaks. There are catcalls and everybody is screaming; some are whistling.

"This is my beautiful wife and I love her with all my heart. You will be hearing three new songs that her love has inspired me to write. I hope you enjoy them and they inspire you to find a love like ours." He looks at me. "I love you, baby." The noise from the audience is deafening, with whistles, screams, shouts, claps, and stomping feet. There are so many camera flashes, it looks like a strobe light going off.

He kisses me again then walks me off the stage. I stand there in the wings and finish watching the concert. The band is great and I am thrilled he has acknowledged our marriage. Maybe it will keep him free from the attention of so many women.

What am I saying? He is absolutely gorgeous, how could they not want to be with him? I understand entirely. It isn't only that he is so handsome, but he is such a sweet, kind, human being and has great humility. Okay, I am unequivocally in love with him. I notice the big beefy guy is standing close. I look at him.

"Security, Mrs. Brand." He acknowledges.

We order room service when we get back from the concert. Some of the band members have chosen to bring girls back to the hotel. They are dressed like normal teenagers and I wonder what they think is going to happen to them. Did they realize these guys were lecherous older men who want sex?

Robbie assures me they are expecting that as a kind of reward. He laughs at me and we don't stay to watch the pairing. He says I am such an ingénue, but that he likes that about me.

We go to our room and have our own party. The hotel bathtub is big enough for two, so we take advantage of it, twice.

I wonder if he is going to do that "introduction thing" at every concert and he says the magazines and star-worthy articles would be out by the morning and sweeping the Internet with the news, he is married. Rolling Stone calls the next day to get the scoop. Robbie meets with the journalist in the afternoon and has lunch with him as he answers questions.

Robbie texts me about fifteen minutes into the meeting and asks me to join them.

The journalist enquires about my name and I tell him, "Well, Robbie calls me baby, sweetness, or darling, however, you can call me Mrs. Brand."

Robbie chuckles and shakes his head at me. He whispers, "Such a handful!"

The journalist smiles, but I can guess he will say something scathing about my response in his article.

Robbie keeps his arm around me and I turn and look at him. He gazes at me sensuously and we forget about the guy sitting across from us. He kisses me, gently at first and then with passionate abandon.

The journalist coughs.

"Sorry," Robbie says, never taking his eyes off me. "She just takes my breath away. Did you hear the new songs?" He stops whatever the journalist was going to ask.

"I was at the concert last night" he says. "But the guys said to forget trying to get an interview with you afterwards, that you were properly espoused and ensconced in your room with an angel from heaven."

"My angel," Robbie says kissing me again.

"When did you get married?"

"Last summer in a beautiful flower garden. But my angel was so breathtaking, nobody noticed the flowers. All I could see were her blue eyes and her heartbreakingly gorgeous spirit." He kisses the ring he has placed on my hand.

Monte, the drummer, walks up and takes a seat.

The journalist turns to him. "Are they really this way when I'm not around?"

"Are you kidding? They can't keep their hands off each other and are always gazing into each other's eyes. It is really sickening!" He laughs, looking at us. "Just teasing Robbie. You know, I wish it was me, right man?"

Gaius and James, both guitarists, walk over and pull up chairs. I am so thankful to be taken out of the limelight.

The journalist is glad to have the entire band to interview. I hear him ask one of the guys what my name is and he said he thinks it's Sweetness or Baby. Another says he heard Robbie called me darling once.

"We just call her Angel or Mrs. Brand."

Robbie snickers.

They never did get my name, which is good because I don't know how I will explain them calling me Opal, if Laura reads the article. Angel is the name that is used in the article and everyone thereafter.

The tour takes us to Vancouver, then Seattle, Japan, and a stop in Hawaii for a vacation. It's nice, but I am already getting tired of living out of a suitcase. We stay in Hawaii about a week and have Laura and Lucy join us before we head down to Australia for a few concert dates. Our next stop is Paris.

We don't have long in Paris, but we have a chance to visit the Eiffel Tower and shop in several designer fashion shops. It is fun to go shopping with Robbie. He doesn't care about money and is very generous.

We've been touring nine months when Laura contacts me. Her cancer has returned. She seems really scared when I talk to her. Our next stop is New York City, so I fly on to Nashville instead.

After texting Preston to get the new alarm code, I find the apartment seems untouched. Our random act of vandalism must have been just that. Nevertheless, something is nagging at me, making me feel uneasy.

My new countertops have been installed and the hardwood floors aren't new, but look like they are refurbished. They must have been under the carpet. I make a mental note to pick up a few rugs.

I open the curtains and let in light. I notice something on the floor and realize there are black rose petals on the floor leading to the bedroom. I slowly follow them and almost faint when I see what waits. The comforter is ripped to shreds and a bloody message is scrawled on the bed.

"You will regret this."

There's a picture of Robbie and me in an embrace on stage; the day he introduced me as his wife. Again, I smell the perfume; so familiar.

Terrified, I phone the police. They do everything police do and promise to be in touch. I can't stay at the apartment, so I get in my little car and head to Preston's house. He and Tess are shocked to hear that the apartment has been vandalized, but he admits he hasn't been there in a couple of months. He calls the alarm company and gets the run around.

I take my bags to Laura's house, in hopes that she will let me stay at her house when she hears about the vandalism. I can't get over how big Lucy has gotten in the months I have been away. She is in first grade and her front teeth are missing.

"Wow," I say to her. "Aren't you getting big!"

"You missed my first day of school." She says.

"I'm sorry, little one. I wish I could have been here." I hand her a bag full of presents.

"Are all these for me?" She is excited.

"Yes. I picked them up from many countries I visited. So, you can see I was thinking about you all the time. Sorry I missed your birthday, Lucy. Would you like to go to the ice cream shop and have another celebration with me?

"Yes! Goody!" she trills.

I leave her going through her gifts and wander into the kitchen where Laura is sitting.

"Dad told me your apartment had been broken into." She looks concerned. "Who do you think would do such a thing?"

"Robbie thinks it might be a crazed fan. I don't know. They broke in on Christmas day too and destroyed a painting I had commissioned for Robbie and vandalized our Christmas tree. They wrote in blood on the painting the same words written in blood on the bed: 'You will regret this.' I'm a little scared. I had to remind the police about the incident with the painting. I haven't told Robbie yet, or he would fly down here to take me away. He's a little over protective sometimes." My smile is weak. "He will insist I have a body guard."

"That may not be a bad idea, Leslie. Your husband is a big deal. Some fans may act on their anger at his marital status."

"I'll tell him soon. In the meantime, can I stay with you and Lucy?"

"You don't even need to ask. I welcome your presence like I would my Mother's. You have her calming effect on me. She would be pleased to know you are with us."

Laura's eyes are bright with unshed tears.

"I think someone saw us that first day and recognized him...." My mind wanders back to that day and Zoe's face pops into my mind. Then I remember thinking I saw her face in the crowd another time. And her perfume...

"Excuse me, but I need to make a call." I walk into the backyard to call Zoe.

"Zoe? Hey it's Opal. Just thinking about you and want to know how you and Lonnie are getting on."

"Opal, I see what you have been up to. Married to

Robbie Brand? Wow, big move! How did you manage that?" Her voice seems normal.

"Oh you saw that did you? Yep, I met him in Guatemala. My husband divorced me and Robbie and I were married last summer."

I hesitate. "You haven't been travelling have you?"

There is silence on the phone.

"Zoe? You there? Hello?"

I try calling back, but the connection will not take; something about the lines being busy. I will try calling again later. Besides, it can't really have been Zoe. She wouldn't have any reason to be here.

The police talk with Preston and the alarm company. They said they didn't know why the alarm wasn't working the day of the break-in. I am allowed to go in and clean the mess so I replace the mattress cover, sheets and comforter.

I am glad to get back to my own place, because Robbie shows up the next day. I tell him about the vandalism and he is ready to hop on a plane that very minute and take me back to Guatemala. I remind him that something strange happened down there also, that almost took my life. It seems to me that someone wants me out of the picture.

He joins Lucy and me at the ice cream shop. She has a good time and is chatting happily about her first day of school. She likes Robbie and wants to sit in his lap. He is so good with her and I tell him I think he will be a wonderful father.

We stay in my apartment, although we are both on edge. In the morning, he contacts his security team and they send two body guards. This is a part of his life and as his wife, I will have to get used to it as well. They are constantly around and we travel everywhere in a large black SUV with tinted windows. I think it screams, *"hey, look over here at the celebrity"* but Robbie says it is better than the consequences of not taking protection seriously.

I go with Laura the next day to her doctor's appointment while Robbie stays at her house to watch for Lucy when she gets off the school bus. He takes his fatherly duties very serious and Lucy looks to him as a father she never had, since Chad died when she was just a baby. Their relationship is a blessing, because I love her more than my own life.

The doctor takes Laura's blood and starts her on a new trial drug. He says the only thing left, if this doesn't work is a bone-marrow transplant. I'm terrified by the news, but Laura seems to take it in stride. She is my only child and I don't want to lose her.

After the appointment, I take her out for coffee and ask her if she has a will. Her eyes fill with tears. "Who will take care of Lucy? Dad is too old and I know Tess doesn't want to be stuck raising a kid."

She's quiet for a while, and then she surprises me. "Would you consider adopting my daughter? I know this is a lot to ask of you and Robbie, but she loves you both."

I hold her hand in mine and lean in to give her a hug. "Don't you worry about it; we will talk to Robbie about it tonight. I can't imagine he'd say no."

Robbie is genuinely touched when Laura makes her request. "We are family, Laura. Of course Leslie and I would take care of Lucy, if the time comes. We should stay positive, because I think you will recover from this, but if the worst happens, of course we will be there for Lucy; we both love her very much."

Robbie has to leave; the band is going on tour again. We make plans to meet up in Miami in a few months.

I try to call Zoe again. She doesn't answer right away, but finally her voice comes on the line. "What happened to you? You didn't call me back." She says, out of breath.

"Why are you breathing so hard? Is this a bad time?"

"No, just didn't have my phone on me. So what's happened?" she asks.

"Don't know. I tried to call you back, but it said the network was busy. Have you been in the States? I think I saw you a couple of times."

"Not me. Must have been my look-a-like. So, how is married life?"

"Wonderful. I love Robbie more than life itself and I think he feels the same. He is the sweetest man I have ever met," I gush.

There is a long silence.

"You still there? Zoe? Hello?"

"Sorry, yeah, I'm still here." Her voice is different. "Call me later. Need to go." She hangs up.

Oddly, I could swear I heard sirens on her call, just like the ones outside my apartment. Could she be here? I run outside to the SUV and knock on the window. Bruce rolls down the window. "Ma'am?"

"Did you see a woman with long black hair outside the apartment, talking on a phone?"

"Yes. Is she of importance?"

"Yeah, I think she is."

CHAPTER 17

The next few months are exhausting for Laura, and I help her with everything I can. Most of my time is spent at her place, caring for both her and Lucy. The new drug she's taking is hard on her, but appears to be making a difference. After several months pass and her strength seems to be returning, I make my way to Miami Beach to see Robbie.

I wade through the paparazzi in front of the hotel. Thankfully, none of them recognizes me without Robbie. I walk into the hotel lobby and inhale; smells rich. Robbie and the gang have the penthouse suite; it doesn't take much persuasion to get the elevator man to take me up to the top floor. I don't even knock on their door before it swings open and Robbie is pulling me into his arms.

"I can't surprise you!" I laugh.

"Nope," he smiles raining kisses all over my face. "I felt your hum the minute you stepped off the elevator."

Suddenly there's a large mass in our personal space. I look up to find a huge bodyguard glaring down at me. Robbie turns to him. "God, back down Titan! This is my wife!"

Titan doesn't apologize, giving me a hard look, and crossing his arms.

"Hey Angel." Gaius waves across the room.

"We missed you girl," Monte smiles and smacks down a card on the table as James lets out an expletive.

"Sorry," James looks my way.

I glance back at Titan as Robbie pulls me into the largest room, closing the door and locking it.

"What's with that guy?" I shiver. "He doesn't like me."

"He doesn't like anyone, but he has been our bodyguard for six years or more."

"This is the first time I've ever seen him. I mean, where was he all those months I toured with the band?"

"Yeah, he took a couple of years off. Forget about him. We have more important things to do than talk about him." Then he pulls me into his arms and lets me know just how much he missed me.

After a long "reminder session" I wiggle away from him and I take his hands in mine. "Do you, by any chance, know a woman named Zoe Panopolou? She's a friend of mine from the clinic in Switzerland. I swear I have seen her twice in the States, watching me in the crowd when I go places. I've tried calling her a couple times and the last time, I heard sirens on the line and outside my apartment. I think she was in Nashville when I called her. The body guards saw her talking on her phone right outside our apartment." "She is a HuMEM, like me." I watch his expression. He's trying to remember something, but fails to connect.

"No," he says, "I can't remember a Zoe, but I have forgotten plenty of people from my heavy drinking days.

"Your heavy drinking days?"

"That is something we haven't discussed. I think I was a heavy drinker at one time, really out of control. That's why I don't touch the stuff now." He wrinkles his brow. "No, I get nothing. Sometimes the memories seem near the surface and about to break free, but then they get erased; like it just disappears."

"My darling," I crooned. "Come here. He lays his head on my breasts. I run my fingers through his hair and massage his scalp.

He turns his head, taking my nipple in his mouth and nudging it to harness. Then he turns kissing every inch of my body before returning to my mouth. He looks into my eyes, and then leans in to my lips, gently touching them with his, running his tongue ever so slightly around their surface. I open them and he lightly touches his tongue to mine then thrusts it into my mouth as a wave of passion washes over my insides, turning them to quivering jelly. Our lovemaking is heightened by our ever-increasing need for each other. When we are both satisfied, I fall asleep wrapped in my lovers arms.

We rise early the next morning, escaping Titan and the reporters and go for a walk on the beach. I have on a sundress and sandals and Robbie looks like he did the first day I saw him on the beach in Guatemala.

We stop at the pier and watch the sunrise. I sit between his legs with my back against his chest and his arms around my middle drawing me closer. He nuzzles my ear and neck, when we hear someone approach. The man is wearing baggy worn pants, flip-flops, and a dirty white t-shirt. His hair is long and oily, graying at the temples. He is unshaven. Eyebrows are thick and look like caterpillars following across his brow. His hand pointed towards us is shaking and he is holding a gun.

Quickly, Robbie pushes me into the water and pulls me under the pier. Although a layer of concrete separates us from the mugger, we are vulnerable in the water. Robbie tells me to ride the waves back to shore. He doesn't release me from his grip and I keep falling, sucking in salty water, and trying to keep up. I glance back and see the man is leaning over the edge. His eyes lock with mine and then he disappears. I know he will be waiting for us at the shore.

"There's Titan." I yell.

Robbie shouts to get his attention. A loud pop sounds and I feel a jerk and pain in my arm. Titan fires his gun and the man goes down. Robbie picks me up and runs with me. Police make their way onto the beach and give him permission to take me to the hospital.

We run along with many others who are terrified, screaming in a panic that there will be more shots coming. And they aren't wrong. We hear more gunshots and the sand kicks up around us as we make it to a taxi. Cop cars arrive as Titan gets in the taxi with us.

Robbie uses my phone to call the hotel and informs the band to stay inside with security. Titan is putting pressure on the wound, but blood is seeping out around his hands.

"Baby, are you shot anywhere else? God let me look at you." Robbie pulls on my legs and gasps at the purple bruises that begin to appear from the sand blasting we got.

"Shit! This is getting ridiculous! Who is doing this, Titan? We need to find this prick!"

The hospital is close and my wound isn't life threatening. Both of our lower legs are covered in purple and red blotches from the spray of bullets hitting the sand.

We leave the hospital as quickly as we can, because even thought my arm is bandaged and hangs in a sling, the nanites have been healing me. We have to get out of there before we can explain my disappearing wounds.

Robbie is beside himself with anger. This is not just a prank; it appears the threats against us have turned into another attempt on my life.

Titan takes us back to the police station where they

question us and take our statements. There were two gunmen; the first shooter is in police custody and they continue to hunt the other perp. It seems the man who shot me had been contacted online to make a hit on Robbie's new wife. Although it seems like a crazed fan, we both know that there was an attempt on my life in Guatemala. Robbie seems to think this all relates to Switzerland, which is something we cannot talk about with the police.

We tell the police our story about the other acts of vandalism and the threats against us. I have pictures of the crime scene on my phone and let the police make copies for their records. I also tell them about the first attack at the coffee farm, making sure we are thorough with all the information on the attacks.

The police theorize that three attacks happened while we were together, and only once when I was on my own. They want to know if Robbie has experienced any unusual accidents or strange happenings when I'm not around. He says he did receive a scarf with a skulls and crossbones pattern with a message after one of his concerts, but he just wrote it off, because they get so many strange things from fans.

The inspector stares at Robbie and then looks at me. "What was this message that came with the scarf?"

"Please let her leave and I'll tell you." He looks at me.

"No Robbie, I want to know. You can't keep things from

me, please."

"*Do the world a favor and choke the bitch!*" he whispers.

I gasped. That's why he hadn't wanted me to know.

"There was also the picture of us when I announced to the world our marriage."

The inspector looks at me. "Well, they are definitely after you," he says simply, pointing to me. He frowns and chews on the inside of his cheek. "Do you have any known enemies? People who would want to harm you?"

"Sir," Robbie interrupts. "She had no enemies until she met me. That can only mean it is someone who believes I should be with them or without her. And let me make it clear, Sir, I can't live without her."

The inspector smiles at Robbie's declaration of love.

"Okay, we'll take it from here, but you should get somewhere safe. Get rid of these phones; I would say they are bugged or tapped. The GPS on these phones can pinpoint your location." He takes my phone and opens it. "And look what I found!" He holds up a tracking device.

"How do they do that? My phone is so thin." I say.

Robbie hands the officer his phone, but there's nothing.

I put my phone back in my purse.

"They probably already have your GPS signature and can track you without this device. If you are going to carry it around, I would turn it off. Better yet, take out the battery. I would still get rid of the phone and carry burner phones for a while. You also have to deal with the fact that everyone knows where you are going to be—the tour schedule is public knowledge?"

Two police officers fly into his office. The inspector holds open his door and ushers us out. He has one of his men take us to another hotel.

Robbie and I are stunned. We don't have an explanation for any of this.

"I know one place we would be safe," I say. "We can go to Switzerland."

"Didn't you tell me you were struck by an arrow when you were there?" he reminds me. "What if it wasn't a coincidence?"

"Now every incident that happens is an attempt to destroy us?"

"Not us, baby; you." He pulls me into his arms and kisses me tenderly.

"When you and the guys go on with the tour, I will go back to Nashville and take care of Laura. Maybe if I leave you alone, they will let us be."

"I will never leave you alone." His eyes tear up. "You are mine to take care of. I won't be without you!"

"They will find us, and if you are with me, you will also be hurt. I can't stand that, Robbie."

"Opal, we'll get new phones, like the officer said. They won't be able to track us."

"Are you kidding? Everyone knows where you will be, your tour dates are public knowledge."

Then I'm in his arms again. "Nothing is going to happen to you. Do you hear me love? I will hire a platoon of body guards to protect you."

We step out of the police car and into the lobby of a hotel. It isn't nearly as nice as the last one, but we don't care as long as we are together. The room will not be in either of our names, so we can't be found.

Robbie asks the hotel concierge to purchase two burner phones for us. Robbie hands him a lot of cash, telling him to have his girlfriend go shopping for me. He gives him my sizes information and asks the concierge to buy a couple pair of Levis and t-shirts for him as well. We purchase some flip-flops at the drugstore next door and then wait in our room, ordering room service.

It will be a while before we can contact the the band. Robbie thinks it is best to disable his phone. We take the SIM cards out as well, but not before I write down some numbers and addresses, I don't know by heart.

We are hungry and dig into the food we have ordered. He makes me drink two colas for the sugar. I tell him that I'm not in shock and that after all I have been through lately, it will take a lot more than a shot to the arm to shock me. "The worst that can happen to me is to be away from you." I confess. "That is the worst."

He rolls me over on the bed and lies on top of me. "That's why we must stick together. I can't be without you either."

"I won't put you in danger." I run my hands through his hair. "I love you too much."

We sleep until there is a knock at the door. Robbie answers it and returns with the things the concierge purchased for us.

By evening, we have been in touch with the band. They have moved out of the penthouse suite and situated in another hotel as well. We let them know that we are the intended targets and that someone is particularly trying to hurt me. When he tells them I've been shot, they freak out; I hear them shouting on the speakerphone. Robbie asks me to calm them down, because they are not listening to him.

"Hey guys, I'm okay. I'm alive anyway. The shooters are in custody." They want to know what the police are going to do to keep me safe and I turn the conversation back over to Robbie. By evening, all my injuries have healed. Robbie's' legs don't have any bruises either.

We have three days off before the band's next concert in town, so I make plans to return to Nashville. We both finally admit we are safer apart for a while, until the police are able to find the culprits responsible.

※ ※ ※ ※ ※

The first week in Nashville, I stay at Preston's house for safety's sake. Tess is visiting a friend in Atlanta. Robbie went on with his tour and keeps in touch with the infuriatingly inferior phones we had purchased. How many times can one connection be lost? The last time, I just screamed in anger.

Preston drags himself in the bedroom in a panic. "What's wrong," He is breathing heavy.

"Damn phone!"

"You gave me a heart attack over a phone? I should paddle your ass!"

"You need a jolt of terror once in a while to stir your lymph system and get rid of toxins." I smile at him.

He sinks into the bed. "Damn woman you're going to be the death of me."

"Dramatic much?" I turn and walk out of the room.

Laura comes over for lunch with Lucy in tow. I decide to move to her house because Preston seems too comfortable with our situation. Everything seems quiet and as long as I stay away from my husband, no one seems to care about me.

Before I leave, I go through the house to find our photo albums. I take the pictures of my parents and grandparents. My personal things, like wedding photos and jewelry, I leave for Laura. There isn't really anything from my old life that I want. I have my mother's ruby heart necklace and her wedding rings.

When we arrive at Laura's, an excited Lucy greets me.

"What are you doing home from school?" I tweak Lucy's red nose.

"Ouch," she holds her nose. "That's why. My nose is red and I can't breathe."

"So, what is this I am reading in the paper about you and Robbie being shot at?"

"The police thought it would be better to bring it out in the open in an effort to discourage whoever is trying to break us up."

"Break you up? It sounds more dangerous than that. What has happened?"

I tell her everything, except the part about the arrow. She looks scared for me.

"Don't worry." I say. "It will all blow over now. The police have everything under control and I believe they are getting closer to figuring out who is doing this. They actually arrested the two men who did the Miami shootings, but not who is behind it. The two men said they didn't have a name or even see the person. They were hired over the Internet."

After our talk, Lucy and I walk out in the garden and discuss flowers that are in bloom. When we go back inside, I paint her nails a light sparkling pink and she is pleased. This is one of the many things on my list that I want to do with Lucy.

Two years ago, I took her to see the Nutcracker. That was the first thing on the list. Next would be ice-skating, then to a movie and dinner. I had so many things I want to do with her and she has endless questions.

As the next year passes, Robbie and I managed to see each other a total of four times. Laura is still, thankfully, in remission and Lucy is turning seven. Preston and Tess are moving to Florida; permanently. Our little family is getting smaller.

Laura is starting a job as a teacher's assistant at the school where Lucy is in second grade. We've settled into a routine. Robbie contacts me through someone we trust and I am meeting him next week in Guatemala. The tour is over and we both want to go home.

CHAPTER 18

It is wonderful to be back in Guatemala. Stephanie greets us with tears, especially Robbie. I know she thinks of him as a son she could never have.

Garrett's indifferent and even a little hostile when I try talking to him. I catch him giving me looks of disdain when Robbie is giving me attention, which is nearly always. I ask Stephanie what is going on with him and she is as surprised as I am. She says she will talk with him.

As life seems to return to normal, I learn how to do many jobs around the farm and even learn how to make espresso and pour designs with the frothy cream. We work all day and make love all night. Robbie and I are very content, until I notice some strange things going on.

The nanites keep sending me strange messages about my body that I am having trouble interpreting. Finally, they give me a picture I understand. I am pregnant and they don't know what to do. I tell them that I am growing a little human inside me. I visualize a tiny spot getting bigger and bigger until it is recognizable as a baby. Then I visualize the baby coming out of me and flip through a calendar of nine months. They are thrilled.

I plan very carefully to tell Robbie. He comes in one evening very disgruntled with something that had happened with the workers. After his shower and a change of clothes, I sit him in a chair and climb into his lap. He lays my head against his chest and sighs.

"I'm sorry you had such a bad day," I say. "You want me to make it better?"

He smiles. "Being with you always makes the day better."

"How about being with two of us? Would that make your day even better?" I am being coy.

"Two of you? Are you telling me you have a twin?" He teases.

"No," I answer.

"Is Lucy here?"

"No, but maybe a Kara or a Sam."

He knits his brows and shakes his head stumped.

"We are pregnant! The nanites just showed me a few days ago, but I wanted to make sure I understood them before I told you."

I watch his expression.

He looks in my eyes. "We're pregnant? We are going to have a baby?"

"Yes."

He pulls up my shirt and rubs my belly.

"Actually, Robbie, it's a bit lower than that." I smile and move his hand down.

"I'm going to be a father?" His smile is stunning and his eyes glisten with unshed tears.

"Every morning they have been giving me a picture of the baby. Well, actually, it is more like a dot in a circle that is my womb. I had to communicate with them by showing them pictures of a dot growing into a full term baby that will deliver in nine months."

He gazes at me with wonder. "You're going to be a great dad."

"They won't kill it?" He asks with trepidation.

"No, I'm the first HuMEM to be able to communicate with them, so they won't hurt it. Actually, I think they are excited."

He smiles and kisses me. "I love you, my Angel. Wow! I'm going to be a dad."

"Can we just keep this to ourselves for a while? I know you are excited, but I really want to wait to tell anyone until I can't keep it a secret. Maybe six months? Please?"

"*By all that is holy, if you think it is best, that is what we will do.*" He says exaggerating his accent.

"I love you, Robbie McCaster. Always."

He keeps his hand down my pants protectively, until I get up to get his dinner. He sniffs the air. "You cooked?"

"Green bean salad, baked rosemary potatoes, and a small piece of grilled fish."

He eats with a relish. "Not only beautiful," he teases, "but useful in the kitchen!" He moves his eyebrows up and down.

"Only the kitchen?" I ask, arching a brow.

"The kitchen, living room, bedroom, bathroom, and everywhere else we can find." He yanks me close and runs his hand up under my shirt, stroking my breasts. His touch makes me melt inside and I can't help but gasp a little, which always seems to make him horny. His lips fund mine and we leave the dishes for later as we undress and step in the shower together.

"This won't hurt the baby will it?" He stopped inches from touching me.

"No." I answer pulling him into me. We make quick work of the love making and washing, and then together we tackle the dishes.

Robbie falls asleep with his arms around me, one draped protectively around my chest and the other hand over his child.

↙ ↙ ↙ ↙ ↙

Garrett's attitude appears to have changed for the better. I manage to give him the benefit of doubt and we all work very hard to ready the farm for the monsoon season, which hits at the end of May. It will rain until October and we will not be able to harvest the coffee cherries or dry them until then. This is the time of year for new plantings and cleanup.

Garrett and Stephanie will be going to the coffee trade shows this year, taking samples of our brew-ready coffees. They will leave at the end of the week and return at the end of October. I am happy to have Garrett out of the way. He's less hostile, but gets on my nerves with his snide remarks to Robbie. I asked Robbie about it and he says it is part of who Garrett is and I will have to accept him.

Before they leave, I hear him speaking to someone on the phone. He is talking about me and saying something about me not being around much longer. Perhaps I've misunderstood, but I'm sure he doesn't like me—maybe he wants me to leave.

I would miss Stephanie, though. She has become like an older sister to me. It is strange to feel younger again, but you can't help it when you are treated that way by everyone you meet.

As the weeks pass, my tummy starts to protrude a bit. I am only two months along, but the pictures the nanites give me in the mornings are showing a bit more than a speck now; more like the tip of a pencil eraser.

Robbie meets the band for two concerts in South

America over the summer. They are only gone for a couple days at a time, but the rest of their concert dates are rescheduled until after the baby is born.

Sometimes I'm tempted to call Dr. Rushing, and other days, I remind myself to stay far away from her. I don't know what she would do if she knew about my pregnancy. I suspect she will do everything she can to lock me up and study me. However, the day might come when I will need her help.

My Spanish is improving and I practice with the women in the kitchen. They all called me Angel after hearing Robbie's nickname for me. Amparo teaches me how to make tortillas and Maria's specialty is paella. It is made with rice, seafood, chicken, pork, and lots of tomatoes, garlic, saffron, and onions.

I stay away from the men as a rule; they all like to touch my hair. Their eyes follow me everywhere I go. It is kind of creepy, but Robbie says I don't have to worry; they respect him and I am his wife, so they will respect me. They only want to look, because I am so beautiful.

A couple of months later, Robbie wants to paint the nursery in the house, although I want to keep the baby in the basinet in our bedroom for the first few months. We delight in shopping for baby things, but I really want to go shopping in the States. He says we will have to move somewhere after the baby becomes school age so he or she can have a proper education. He wants to move to England. I want to be near

Lucy, so our child can grow up close to her.

Robbie won't let me be around the paint and sends me to put together a crib in another room. While I am crawling around on the floor, I feel a little movement.

"Robbie!" I shout.

He runs to my side and helps me up. "What's wrong? Are you okay?"

I am smiling. "The baby moved."

"Really?" His eyes lit up.

"It wasn't a big movement, something like a butterfly's wings."

The nanites are showing me too. I chuckle and send back a picture of a baby sucking its thumb, moving around in a womb, and kicking. They are encouraging more pictures. Robbie watches. He has seen this exchange before, so he knows I am communicating with them.

I smile and look at him. "They are finally giving me moving pictures." I let the tears fall.

"Is everything alright with them?" he asks.

"Perfect. I sent them memories of a video I saw recently about the movements of a baby in the womb. They are learning how to send such pictures back to me. I can see our baby as it moves."

"Awesome! I wish I could see the pictures." His hand cups my growing tummy and his eyes sparkle. "I better get that room finished." He turns to leave. "Can they tell what gender it will be?"

"I can ask." I close my eyes and ask.

"We are going to have a girl."

"Kara," he whispers in amazement. "Our darling little Kara. Daddy's little girl." Robbie gets down on his knees and kisses my belly when there is a knock at the door. He jumps up and opens it. "Stephanie? What are you doing home?"

She pushes past him and takes in the scene. "Are you pregnant?" She is looking at my belly. "Oh my God! You are pregnant!" she exclaims, hugging me.

"Four months," I say. "The nanites can show me moving pictures of the baby. They are fascinated and have just told me we are having a little girl."

"Congratulations!" She hugs Robbie. "How absolutely marvelous! I'm going to be a grandmother, sort of." She scratches at some paint on Robbie's face. "You will have to change that color to pink." She laughs.

"Actually, we decided to paint it in diagonal pastel stripes with white shadow pictures," he says. "It could be a boys or girls room."

"We will make sure the bed skirt and draperies are pink though." I add.

"When is the big day?" she asks.

"It should be sometime in late January or early

February." Robbie says. "We are a bit vague on the exact day of conception, but we know the day the nanites told us."

"No kidding, the way you two go at sex, I don't doubt it would be difficult to pinpoint an exact date." She laughs.

Robbie looks at me and grins. He put his arms around me and leans in to kiss my cheek.

"Your boobs are about to pop out of that top aren't they?" she observes.

I look down and frown. "I haven't really thought about them. Huh. I don't wear a bra most days so I didn't realize they were growing. But now that you've said it, I can see they are bigger."

Robbie's eyes are locked on my boobs, so Stephanie steps up and snaps her fingers. He looks up and laughs.

"Just taking in the scenery."

"Uh huh." She laughs.

CHAPTER 19

Garrett didn't return with Stephanie and I am grateful for his absence. The three of us have dinner in the hotel dining room and then we walk Stephanie to her house to make sure she is going to be okay by herself. We tell her she can stay with us until Garrett returns, but she wants to sleep in her own bed.

Robbie gives me a thorough examination when we get back home. He is miffed that he missed the fact my breast size has increased and he hasn't noticed. I tell him a watched pot never boils and he says that doesn't have anything to do with breast size. I laugh and suggest that the lesson learned is that as long as you are looking at them every day, you won't notice the small changes.

He makes love to me as he does every night and falls asleep with his head on my breast. I wake up to his suckling at my breast, before his hand finds his favorite toys and invites me to play. When we are finished, he lays with his ear on my swelling belly listening intently to see if he can hear his daughter. I feel a gurgle, but he isn't sure if he heard it or not.

We dress for the day and I decide to wear an exercise

bra for additional support and the biggest shirt I own. I will eventually have to get some new bras and maternity clothes.

I talk to Laura later in the day and ask her to send me some maternity clothes and a few bras. She gasps when I tell her my bra size. She is so excited to hear that we are pregnant. I tell her we are going to have a girl and will name her Kara.

She says Lucy is doing well in school, but that Laura herself is feeling very tired lately. I ask if she has been to the doctor and she says her regular three-month appointment is coming up soon. I tell her not to worry, that there are periods in a woman's life that are more tiring than others. Of course, neither of us mentions the dreaded disease. For the moment, we pretend it doesn't exist.

She says Preston's house has been sold and she asks if there is anything I need or want from the house. I tell her I will take the outdoor furniture if she doesn't want it. She says she would put it on my deck at the apartment.

I ring off in good spirits. How I miss them. I have a short cry and even think about Preston and cry some more. I mourn my own death for a few days...my past life. Must be those pregnancy hormones!

Robbie and Stephanie come in while I am trying to stop crying. He is concerned that I am crying so much. "Yesterday you cried over a turtle that had been run over in the drive way. Are you sure you are okay?"

"It's just my hormones, Robbie. It is normal for a pregnant woman to have emotional flare-ups. It doesn't mean anything. Ask Stephanie if you don't believe me. Goggle it or something!" I shout and stomp off leaving him staring after me, his mouth hanging open.

I know Stephanie will tell him not to worry, but I feel bad I yelled at him. What is wrong with me? I don't want to be around him right now. My emotions flex from happy, to sad, to anger. I can't seem to control them. I am so worried I will hurt my husband with my outbursts.

When I return to the house, he is sitting on the couch with the stereo playing the new album he had recorded a few months ago. I recognize one of the new songs.

"Trying to convince yourself you still love me?" I tease. "I'm so sorry Robbie," I sit on his lap.

He nuzzles my neck. "It's okay, love. You can't help it. I understand that. I'm just worried about you."

He looks into my eyes until he feels the connection and then sighs with relief.

"What is that all about? Think I've gone off you?" I caress his face.

"Making sure we are in sync. This little hum between us is so satisfying; it keeps me centered." He confesses. "I've noticed several times, when you seem to be angry with me the hum disappears. It scares me."

"Maybe the baby interferes with our hum. I am its mother and I'm sure it has an electrical frequency it operates at. It could be interfering with ours. After all, we don't know what is going on at the moment."

"You have about four more months before you deliver. If things don't right themselves soon, I want you to consider contacting Dr. Rushing." He holds my gaze. "Now, I know that isn't what you want to hear, but I really think she may have some answers for us."

"The Dragon Lady. Yes, I'm thinking the same. I'll call her if I start feeling weird again." I promise. "But only as a last resort."

Everything goes smoothly for the next two weeks. I receive a wonderful package of pregnancy clothes and underwear from Laura. She also sent a bed set as a shower gift. It is a frilly pink crib skirt with ribbon roses. The crib sheets are white with embroidered white roses. She included a mobile from Lucy and sent me some of her school pictures. Lucy is getting so big and is now eight and growing into a lovely girl. She has long dark brown hair. I wonder what happened to the strawberry blonde hair she had as a toddler?

Over the next week, I become sex starved. I want it every time I see Robbie. He is very happy to oblige at first, but I think I wear him out. He falls asleep after every encounter and although I know this is not abnormal behavior for me, I think maybe that is how the nanites are regulating my hormones, because I feel more like myself than I have in a month.

I am asleep the next time Robbie comes into the bedroom. He leans in to kiss me and I feel extreme pain all over my body. I jump up and run in the kitchen. "Stay in there!" I say. "You are hurting me." I leave and walk to Stephanie's.

She opens the door and quickly yanks me inside. "What are you doing over here? Did you have a fight?"

"Call Robbie on the phone, I need to talk to him!" I cry.

He answers quickly. "Stephanie, is Opal over there? She screamed at me and ran out the door. Told me to stay away, that I was hurting her."

"It's me Robbie. I'm sorry love, but our hum is off again and being around you is causing me pain. It makes my whole body hurt. I'm trying to communicate with the nanites and find out what is happening. I love you, Robbie. Please understand."

"I'm so worried about you, Opal. Can you put Stephanie on the phone?" He insists. "Stephanie, please watch over her. I think we are going to have to make that trip to Switzerland. Call me if there are any more complications."

I sit very still and try to get the nanites to tell me why I experience pain when I am with Robbie. I show them a picture of his face and a picture of my body with my face in pain with a question mark.

The answer they give is one I don't want to see. The baby is putting out a different frequency than we do. They show me that the frequency keeps changing and they don't know when it would become stationary. There is nothing we can do, but wait it out. I ask them to let me know when the frequency changes again.

I call Robbie to let him know. "Robbie, darling, it's the baby. The nanites are telling me that her frequency keeps altering and that they don't know when it will become stable. They will let me know when it is back to normal. Until then, my love, you are on your own. Besides," I tease, "after last week you could probably use the rest."

He chuckles in his sexy voice. "We'll take it a day at a time. You are near six months now. We have to decide where to have this baby. You can't fly after seven months, even if we fly now it will be a risk."

"We can fly part of the way one day and the rest of the way another day." I say.

"I Googled it." He snorts. "Long haul flying isn't recommended at all during pregnancy. So we'll go first class, when Kara changes her frequency again. In the meantime, we'll take turns packing."

"Okay. I'll call Dr. Rushing tonight." I say, resigned.

"I miss you, Angel." He hangs up.

Stephanie hands me her phone book. This is one phone call I am dreading making. I can't stand The Dragon Lady on the best of days. She seems so wrapped up in her own little world of control and seizing every opportunity she can to complicate my life. I have no doubt that somehow she is the one trying to do me in.

Turning to her for help is compromising my freedom and I need to remember to remain as emotionally distant as I can from her. Zoe is another matter completely. I can't figure out what she is doing in Nashville. Why would it be such a secret? We were such good friends before I left the clinic. We spent a lot of time together travelling around Europe and sharing new experiences. If she wanted to visit me, she only need let me know she is on her way.

"Dr. Rushing, this is Opal. I'm pregnant and having a bit of trouble. Can you call me back at Stephanie's? Thank you." I hang up. "Voice mail."

"Here," Stephanie hands me a cup of chamomile tea. "She'll call as soon as she gets the message."

The phone rings soon after. Stephanie answers.

She hands the phone to me. "Hello?"

I sit quietly while I listen to Dr. Rushing shooshing everyone who is talking. "What is happening?" she asks. "How far along are you and who is the father?"

"My husband is the father. I'm sure you know who that is, like everyone else in the world. I'm six months pregnant and I have no other way to tell you than the baby's frequency is causing problems."

"It's frequency?" She asks.

"Yeah, like Robbie and me kind of 'hum' when we are together. Our frequencies are very compatible, but the baby's frequency keeps changing and when it does, I have intense pain all over my body anytime Robbie is near me."

"Who told you about the baby's frequency?"

"The nanites." I say, very matter of fact, revealing my secret. "They let me know when I conceived and have been keeping an eye on things. We are communicating. Every morning they show me a moving picture of my Kara."

She has me on speakerphone and everyone is talking at once. "I knew they didn't all leave! Shoosh it or get out!" She shouts. "When can you come here, Opal?"

"Not until Kara's frequency changes and I can be around Robbie again. I won't leave without him."

"Okay," she says, "but don't wait too long. We need to get you here where we can monitor everything. You are the first HuMEM to become pregnant and I'm shocked you've reached your sixth month. I don't need to tell you how excited we all are to see you."

"I'll call you when we know we'll be travelling."

"No," she says, "don't call. I don't want a record of when you fly. We'll be waiting." She hangs up.

"Weird," I say to Stephanie. "She doesn't want a record of when we fly? What's that all about?"

"Sounds ominous," She remarks, her brows pull together. "Who knows? That woman is off her rocker sometimes."

"I'm tired. Where can I sleep?"

She takes me by the hand and leads me to the guest bedroom. "Will this do?"

"Yep, as long as it has a bed." I sniff. "I miss Robbie."

"Yeah, you two haven't been apart for months now. And especially after last week!" She laughs.

"He told you?" I ask, red faced. "Well, to be quite honest, I was rather horny when I was pregnant with Laura too."

She laughs and shuts the door.

It takes eight days for the baby's frequency to change. I rush to see Robbie before he is even out of bed and crawl up beside him without any clothes. It doesn't take him long to catch on and we have wonderful reunion sex. Hot, steamy, and much needed by both of us. He strokes my belly, talking to Kara and lays his head to listen when he feels a movement under his cheek.

"I felt her!" He jumps on the bed then lays back down to

listen again. He is like a kid with a new toy. "Oh wow!" Tears run out of his eyes. "So what's that like for you, having something kicking you on the inside?" He laughs. "Marvelous. Absolutely marvelous."

"Well," he jumps off the bed and drags me to my feet, "time for a shower and we need to get dressed and get on our way. Wanna stop off in Nashville to see Lucy and Laura?"

"Oh, can we? Yes, I would love to do that." He is trying to please me in every way possible. I reach up and kiss him letting him know how much I know he is trying.

He quickly showers and then helps me, bending down to wash my feet and legs. Soaping my belly and crooning some song he'd been working on for Kara. He kisses me tenderly before passion takes hold of both of us and we are having sex. The hot and heavy ends as the water turns cold and we both run squealing from the shower.

Our bags are packed and ready to travel. We stop at Stephanie's and hand her the keys to our house. She says Garrett is on his way home and will arrive tonight. She assures us she will take care of everything like always. Robbie and I kiss her goodbye and make our way to the taxi.

"Bring back a healthy baby!" She calls.

CHAPTER 20

Lucy is gangly now with long legs that have all kinds of scrapes and bruises. "How did you bang up your legs?" I ask.

"I trip a lot and one time I fell off my bike. That's this one," she points to a scab on her knee. "Oh and I'm learning to skate."

I smile and tweak her nose. "I love you." I say pulling her in for a hug.

"Why is your belly getting so big?" She wrinkles her nose.

"Leslie is going to have a baby, remember?." Laura tells her.

"You look so lovely, Leslie. You positively glow!" Laura smiles. "I wish you were staying for a while."

Laura does not look well and I ask her to walk with me in the backyard. "What did the doctor say?"

"The tests are inconclusive. They say it could be Leukemia. My blood tested positive for M-spike protein."

I gasp and she hangs her head. "Laura. Oh my darling girl!" I tug her in for a hug. "I'm sure they are wrong. I am thinking maybe it is Adrenal Fatigue Syndrome. Would you consider going to a homeopathic doctor? I will make the appointment."

"Sure," she agrees. "A second opinion wouldn't hurt."

"A third and fourth opinion wouldn't hurt either." I say smiling. "Just keep getting opinions until you find one you like."

She lets me hold her, until Lucy comes running up to us and captures our attention with her antics. She is in cheerleading and wants to show me some routines she is learning.

We stay three days in Nashville. It is enough time to say hello, make an appointment for Laura with the naturalist I had mentioned, and say goodbye. She promises to keep in touch and let me know what she finds out.

Robbie and I room at the apartment those three days. We go by the artist's house to see why we haven't received our repaint. He proceeds to tell us that he has had to contact the police because there was a break-in and the painting was stolen. I ask why he didn't paint it from the picture that was still in his possession. The sound of a drawer opens and he hands me a note.

"REPAINT THE LOVER'S PICTURE AGAIN AND I'LL KILL YOU!"

Robbie sucked in his breath. "We'll stop by the police station and talk with them." He shakes the artist's hand. "If this is evidence, how do you still have it?" Robbie asks.

"I just received it a couple days ago. Someone has also left me a number to phone, but when I did, there wasn't anybody there." He explains.

I take the note and promise to deliver it to the police when we go there, along with the phone number.

"Let me have the photo." I hold out my hand and put it in my purse. I want to have it painted some day when all this is behind us.

⊬ ⊬ ⊬ ⊬ ⊬

Robbie arranges for us to fly into Austria and take a helicopter up the mountain to the clinic. I am not too enthusiastic about the helicopter ride. It is loud and not as smooth a trip as I hoped it would be. Robbie enjoys the ride immensely.

When we arrive, Dr. Rushing starts in immediately. She wants to check my vitals, but I just want to rest. I let her take my weight, listen to the baby's heartbeat, and take my blood pressure, but I refuse any other prodding until I sleep. She's has a room prepared for us.

Many technicians gather to get a look at my pregnant belly. There are more than a few interested in Robbie's presence.

"Where's Zoe?" I question the doctor.

"Don't know. She left here several summers ago; a

private matter. She wouldn't tell me anything."

"Is Lonnie with her?"

"No. She just up and disappeared." She says.

So, it is very probable that I had seen her those times and that she was in Nashville during the phone call when I could have sworn she was outside my apartment. What could that mean? I need to talk to Lonnie.

"Now tell me about the frequency thing."

"Tomorrow, please. I'm so exhausted," I say.

She sighs. "You're right. You need your rest.

In our room, Robbie runs a bath for me and helps me out of my clothes and into the marble tub. He washes my hair and bathes me while singing the new lullaby he wrote for Kara. Then he helps me into some pajamas and into our bed. He knows I am tired, so he holds me and nuzzles my neck until we both fall asleep.

I sleep late the next morning. Robbie is awake and dressed, watching the news. He hears me stretch and make waking up noises.

"You had a good night's sleep." He says. "I'll see if I can scrounge up something for you to eat." He kisses me tenderly and kisses my belly. "Both my girls are safe. I love you angels."

"I'm surprised Dr. Rushing hasn't been here already." I say.

"She was and I ran her off. I told her that she can wait

until you are awake and have breakfast."

"My Hero! Wow, I could have used you the entire time I was trying to deal with her and Zoe!" I laugh.

"Ah," he says, "and where is this Zoe you keep talking about?"

"Dr. Rushing said she left the clinic several summers ago. Now I'm wondering if I did see her in Nashville. Very strange." I remember the angry look on her face.

He kisses me and leaves. I am dressed when he returns with a tray containing a decaf coffee latte, a bowl of fruit salad, and some muesli. I grab the coffee first.

"You spoil me!" I grin.

"I want to spoil you; both of you!" He brushes my hair.

Dr. Rushing knocks and walks in without waiting for an invitation. We will have to remember to lock that door. She takes in the scene.

"Brushing her hair? Aren't you sweet!" Her tone is acidic.

I turn to look at her. "You need an attitude change doctor," I say. "If you can't treat either one of us with respect, we can leave."

She sniffs and looks down at the floor. "Sorry, I'm just anxious to get started and your husband made me leave."

"You need to understand that she is in a delicate condition and has had a harrowing journey to get here. Please, don't risk my wife or my baby's lives or I will take them away." Robbie is polite, but firm.

"Agreed. Now, is it possible to get an ultra sound?" she asks.

"Eww. I hate that gel stuff." I stand up. "Can you warm it up? It's so cold!"

"Yes, I know it is your favorite thing." Dr. Rushing finds her humor and smiles.

"Come, Robbie, I want to see our daughter." I take his hand. "This will be exciting!"

Dr. Rushing gives Robbie a grimace, but turns and walks ahead of us.

People stop and watch us in the halls. I keep hearing them say things like 'Is that Robbie Brand?' 'Wonder what he is doing here?' That's his new wife, Angel.' 'Look, she is pregnant.'

Dr. Rushing ushers us into the clinic. "Well, you two are certainly the talk this morning!" She chuckles.

"Yeah," I say. "We get that a lot."

Robbie pulls me to him and kisses me. As usual, he leans in and nuzzles my neck, which sends shivers all over my body. He holds me close.

Dr. Rushing turns around and says I can hop up on the examination table and expose my tummy.

Robbie lifts me up; she grimaces again.

The doctor pulls the machine over and a table with a monitor, so we can watch what the wand reveals.

Kara's little spine looks like a necklace of pearls. We can see her tiny feet and hands. She is puckering her lips, like she is going to kiss. Her head is beautiful and round.

"She has your ears, baby." Robbie smiles.

He is transfixed, in complete awe and asks the doctor if she is recording it. She says she is and will give us a copy.

"And yes, it is a girl!" Dr. Rushing beams.

"Our little Kara," I am crying.

"Kara." Dr. Rushing repeats. "Nice name."

The Doctor is a little misty eyed too.

"She looks very healthy and is the proper weight. I do believe she will be born late January or early February as the nanites have indicated by the conception date." She is writing in her book. "So let's get you cleaned up and we'll have that talk. I'll be in my office."

She pokes her head out of the examination room door and shouts at the crowd waiting for information. "It's a girl, healthy, and at least at the end of the 2nd trimester. Get back to work everyone!"

Robbie looks at me and shrugs his shoulders.

"Now," she begins, "tell me about this frequency phenomenon you spoke about."

"When I first met Robbie at a restaurant and he

touched me, I felt a current run through me. Actually, the entire restaurant felt the current. Everyone was rubbing their arms, like all the hair was standing up on their arms. Then every time we saw each other the current started settling into a hum. I don't know that it is anything anybody else can hear, but it has become a comforting part of being a couple." I nod to Robbie.

"Are you feeling that hum now?" she looks confused.

"Yes," Robbie said taking my hand and playing with my ring. "If I walk out of the room, I'm not sure how far I will get before it will break."

"Let's try it," she says.

Robbie smiles at me and kisses my head. "See you in a minute."

Dr. Rushing rolls her eyes.

He walks out of the room and down the hall. I let her know when the hum stops and she yells at him to stop. She goes to see how far he went. I heard his footsteps start returning and tell her it's back. He smiles when he walks back in the office and retakes his seat, grabbing my hand and kissing it.

"Okay," she says, "I admit there is something happening with you two, but what happened with the baby?"

"Can we agree that the biological composition of the human body operates by electrical impulses? The heartbeat operates at 2hz if it beats at 120 bpm and we process visual stimuli at 60hz. All of our nerves function with electrical impulses, as well as our brains. Somehow, Robbie and I are symbiotic. Together, we create a sort of energy field.

I have come to understand that the baby's energy frequency is in flux at the present and will eventually settle into a frequency that is normal for her. However, she has in the past interfered with the harmony between our 'hum'. I have experienced excruciating pain all over my body whenever Robbie was around me. It lasted for about a week. The nanites let me know when the frequency changed back to one that wouldn't harm me," I finish.

Dr. Rushing stares at us, listening intently. "We shall test this."

"Not if it is going to disturb Kara." Robbie says.

"No, of course not," Dr. Rushing says. "We are going to measure this energy field. This is totally fascinating. It could explain a lot of the problems we had with some HuMEMs."

"I want to share something else I have become aware of with my music which also operates on different frequencies, depending on which notes are played. That is how music can heal a body," I explain.

"Sickness and disease can interrupt the normal frequency of a person's body. If we play songs that produce certain sound waves, we can readjust the body's frequency and kill disease. A song in a minor chord can have an effect on the nervous system and bring about a deliverance of negative energy. It is possible to use radio frequency to promote tightening of the skin. We know this for a fact. It is the sound waves and energy field that creates a harmonious frequency for the body.

What Robbie and I experience is on an exaggerated level, but normal for all animals who find their mates."

"Not only beauty, but brains too." Robbie smiles.

"Any musician can attest to this: If you take the songs that have been your most popular and compare the general chords that are played, I bet you will find they are all the same. Then those songs that you have wondered why they weren't appreciated as much were in chords that produced anxiousness, agitation, and discord." I continue, looking at Robbie.

"That is something I will be looking at closer when I get the chance," he says. "To think you have all this information and we haven't discussed this phenomenon!"

"Why haven't you?" Dr. Rushing asks.

"Well, when we are together, we are into each other; if you get my drift." Robbie stares at my face, smiling.

"Please, spare me the details!" Dr. Rushing scowls.

She stands up and walks towards the door. "I will be in touch when the test is ready. In the meantime, enjoy the spa and when you go outdoors be mindful of your surroundings."

"What do you mean by that remark?" I ask confused.

"Well, this is the same time of year when you were shot with an arrow; hunting season has begun here. We do everything we can to keep out the hunters, but you can never be completely sure." She says and leaves.

Robbie and I stare after her then looking at each other. I see we have the same expression of fear. "What was that all about?" he asks. "Were you shot with an arrow here at the Spa? That sounds like a threat to me. Will she try to hurt you?"

"You don't remember me telling the police about the incident with the arrow?" I ask. "Or maybe I didn't tell them. I think I did. Yeah, I was outside sitting in the gardens and when I stood up from the bench, an arrow went in my right thigh. If I hadn't stood up when I did, it would have hit me in the back and went through my heart."

Robbie's look is complete shock. "Why did we come back here? Someone was trying to kill you even then?"

"The grounds keeper believes it was an accident by a hunter who had wondered into the Spa's private grounds, saw movement and aimed for what they thought was a deer; until they heard me scream. He never found the hunter though." I explain.

"What if it wasn't an accident?" He hugs me close.

"We don't have a choice, Robbie. We have to think of

Kara now." I say defeated.

"There is no way we can stay cooped up in this clinic for three months Opal."

"I did, Robbie. Sure, I took small vacations with Zoe during that time, but most of it was spent right in this spa."

"I don't know....there is something creepy about this place. I feel really weird and Dr. Rushing is always looking at me strangely. She doesn't like me or approve of me."

"Please," I snicker. "She is strange most of the time. I think it is because she has a one-track mind. This is only our first day here, let's give it some time." I plead. "Besides, you stand in her way of total control over me and our daughter."

"Best not let our guard down."

"Maybe we can go to Zoe's cabin on the Boden Sea. It is so peaceful there. I'm sure you will love it. Maybe Lonnie knows how to get in touch with her."

"Lonnie?"

"He's her husband. I wonder if he left the clinic with Zoe? Surely she wouldn't leave him."

We have the rest of the week to ourselves. Robbie starts working out in the gym to fill his days while I fill his nights. We take a SUV down to Tuefen and explore the small town. Nothing happens and we feel relieved to be away from the spa for a few hours. The air on the mountain is crisp and clean and the village offers everything that is unique about a

Swiss village.

I see Lonnie on Saturday and corner him. He gives me a hug and congratulates me on being pregnant. He sadly tells me that Zoe left him to find someone. He supposes she is in Greece, where she is from.

"Have you heard from her at all?"

He shakes his head. "No, Opal. Nothing. One day she was here and everything was fine. The next day she packed her bag and left. No explanation. Just gone."

He is heartbroken.

"Do you think she would mind if we spent a month at the cabin?"

"Sure you can spend time there. It's really my place. Let me get you the key." He walks down the hall and returns a few minutes later and hands me the key. "I'll make sure everything is winterized. Have fun."

I leaned forward and give him a hug. He carefully leans in trying to hug around my tummy. He smiles and kisses my cheek.

"Really happy for you and Robbie."

"Thank you, Lonnie. I'm sure Zoe will come back soon." I try to console him.

Dr. Rushing starts her barrage of tests on Monday. She is relentless and Robbie keeps a close eye on what is happening. Twice he stops the tests completely and won't allow them. He feels they will hurt Kara or myself. I love the way he takes control. Dr. Rushing doesn't. She is always complaining about him under her breath, but loud enough for everyone to hear her.

On Thursday, I had enough of her mouth and let her know that we will be leaving the clinic for a trip to the cabin for at least a week. She is livid and shouting that she can't allow that.

"We came here on our own and we can leave on our own. You can't tell us what we can and can't do. So if you don't want us to come back, let me know now and we can fly home and to hell with you!" I shout backing her up against the wall. "I'm not some damn experiment! What happened to me was not my fault! You don't own me, woman! So back off, now!"

"Okay," she acquiesces. "But I insist you have protection. I'll make the arrangements."

✌ ✌ ✌ ✌ ✌

Robbie and I leave the next morning. Our time at the Sea is wonderful. Titan shows up the day after we arrive. Robbie felt it necessary to have his own security. We make love and talk about our lives with each other. Our time together, since we have met was mainly filled with sex and quiet times. We took a trip to a town to buy supplies and realize that Dr. Rushing actually hired people to watch after us, without interfering.

I keep in touch with Laura every few days. She is scheduled to take series of chemotherapy drugs starting as soon as the holidays are over. I am very sad that my daughter is ill and I can't go to her and be myself. I cry myself to sleep most nights. Robbie says that as soon as Kara is born we will go to Nashville and we can take care of her.

We stay at the cabin until after the Christmas holiday. I have returned to the clinic every week for a checkup and according to Dr. Rushing, everything is going to plan, including the Braxton Hicks contractions I am experiencing. When it first happened, Robbie and I panicked. But then I remembered my first birth and was able to relax, knowing it was normal.

We return after New Year's Day to stay in the room that was assigned to us. Several weeks before my due date, I wake up to an excruciating pain radiating all over my body. We know what has happened; the baby's frequency has once again shifted. Robbie moves into another room down the hall. We are both miserable being away from each other. We talk to each other over the internet and wait for another change in frequency.

Late on January 29th, I go into labor. The baby's frequency hasn't changed and Robbie isn't able to see the birth of his daughter except for the monitor set-up in his room. There are three cameras stationed around the bed where the delivery is taking place. Dr. Rushing wants to record everything about it.

I try to communicate with the nanites during the birth of Kara, so they won't interfere. They ask numerous questions, but tend to make a nuisance of themselves when I am trying to breathe during contractions. Dr. Rushing doesn't administer the favored epidural to block pain and cause temporary paralysis. She says it isn't known how the nanites will react to such medication, so I suffer a natural birth.

Dr. Rushing becomes distraught as my blood pressure drops dramatically. "Opal," she pleads. "Please open your eyes, you must stay awake. The baby needs your help to be born." She shakes me and I look into her eyes. "Push!"

I scream as the next contraction hits me and push with all I have in me.

"Again! Push! Come on girl; we have to get Kara out of the birth canal."

"I can't! I'm too tired!" I complain.

"Robbie, you need to talk to her!" Dr. Rushing shouts towards the cameras.

"Hey baby!" His voice echoes in the room. "You can do this. We have been waiting for our darling Kara. She can't wait to see her Mommy. You need to push, baby."

"I'll try, Robbie."

Seconds later, I hear a cry and pass out.

Robbie's head is lying on the bed next to my hip when

my eyes open. I smile remembering that Kara was born. I comb my fingers through his hair when he looks up and smiles at me, except it doesn't reach his eyes. A sickening feeling settles deep in my stomach.

The nanites give me a picture of the baby's birth with a question mark. I sit up and look around the room. "Where's Kara, Robbie?"

Tears pool in his eyes. "Opal," he picks up my hand and brings it to his lips placing a kiss in my palm. "I was so worried about you."

"Robbie, where is our baby?" My breath comes in gasps.

"She didn't make it." His tears flow.

"No, no, no. I heard her cry! She was fine." I sob.

Robbie picks me up and puts me on his lap. "Baby, I'm so sorry. She stopped breathing shortly after birth."

Again, the nanites ask about Kara's birth.

"I want to see her. I want to hold her." I stand up and move to the door.

He follows me into Dr. Rushing's office. She isn't there.

I'm looking for someone to talk to and find Heike in the lab. "I want to see my baby. I want to hold her."

Heike looks startled. "What? I mean, you can't!"

"Why?"

"Let me talk to Dr. Rushing. She will know what to do."

Dr. Rushing walks up behind us. "If you will follow me,

I'll take you to her."

I am still facing Heike who raises her eyebrows at Dr. Rushing and looks confused.

"We have a small refrigerator that we use for a makeshift morgue. She's in here."

We hold our baby, Kara, and say our goodbyes. I cry until I finally exhaust myself. Robbie helps me back to the bedroom where I sleep through to the next morning. Robbie has made the funeral arrangements and we bury her in a small cemetery in the quaint city of Teufen.

All the while, the nanites keep a stream of questions about Kara's birth flowing through my mind. They are driving me crazy.

I know Dr. Rushing would have liked to keep our precious one to dissect and experiment on, but we want her small little body kept whole and untouched by her hands. I am surprised she readily agrees. Maybe she has a heart after all.

CHAPTER 21

We leave a week later for Nashville. Laura needs me. I have another baby waiting for her momma and I'm not going to disappoint her. She needs my encouragement to help her through this difficult time. Lucy needs her grandmother. I struggle whether to tell them the truth about who I am, but decide to wait and see how it all plays out.

We take a taxi to the apartment. After knowing that someone is trying to kill me, it is difficult to return, but we decide to take our chances. The apartment seems to be as it should. We walk down to the corner market and buy a few things. The winter weather isn't too cold. There isn't any snow, although I think it would be warmer if it did. As it is, the cold is bone chilling, and my cheeks feel like they have been slapped, by the time we make it back home.

Robbie understands why I want to come back to Nashville, but I'm positive he would like to go back to Guatemala.

Alone at last, we struggle to hold our feelings together over the loss of our baby girl. It is a pain that won't leave either of us for a very long time. I can't understand what has happened and neither can the nanites. They keep up their barrage of questions concerning her birth. I wonder if Kara had been endowed with nanites or if they had read her DNA and tried to help with her development. These are questions that will never be answered.

We meet Laura the next morning. I am shocked by her appearance. She is extremely thin and her eyes are dull and her skin grey. "My darling girl!" I pull her into my arms.

"I'm so sorry about your baby girl, Leslie." She cries with me. "It must be horrible to lose a child on its day of birth when you are so excited to finally see her and hold her. Please accept my heartfelt sadness."

"Yes, you do understand what Robbie and I experienced. Thank you for your kind words. I'm just happy I have you to look after now. It will help me with the everyday struggle to cope with her loss." I hug her again. I can feel her bones in her shoulders and her vertebrae feel very pronounced. When she turns and I keep my arm around her waist, I can feel her hip bones. She is already wasting away. Whether it is the disease or the chemotherapy, I don't know.

"How are you feeling, Laura?" Robbie asks.

"Some days are better than others. I tried several chemo pills before the doctors decided the ones I'm on now are better." She sits in the recliner and I can see she is exhausted. Her eyes close and she immediately falls asleep.

I find a roast to make for dinner. I send Robbie to the store to buy a few items, while I sort laundry and start picking up Lucy's bedroom.

Laura slept a good two hours before stirring. "What are you doing?" She asks as Robbie peels potatoes over the sink.

"I'm on KP duty." He laughs.

"Where is Leslie?"

"I'm in here Laura," I say scrubbing out Lucy's tub. "I'm almost finished in here."

She stands in the doorway. "I didn't invite you here to clean my house."

"I'm sincerely glad to be of help. Now why don't you go supervise Robbie in the kitchen? He needs to peel the carrots and garlic."

She laughs. "Wow! The lead singer of *Inventing Abbey* peeling potatoes in my kitchen! Who would have believed it?"

She walks back in the living room as I start dusting. "He's rather handsome. I think I'm star-struck! Lucky you!"

"Me too!" I said glancing his way. He stands engrossed in his work. His hair needs a trim as it curls on his collar. He has on faded jeans and a t-shirt that hugs his muscular chest. The Celtic tattoo he has on his right arm runs from his shoulder to the middle of his bicep and is visible through the thin layer of his white shirt. He wears worn cowboy boots and is belting out a song he is working on. He glances my way when our hum flares. It does this when we are experiencing strong emotions. His eyes lock on mine and he smiles that crooked grin I love.

I walk to him and let my arms encircle his waist, feeling his tight abs and laying my head against his back. I love listening to him sing this way. His voice reverberates all through me and I feel so comforted. I stand on tiptoes and kiss his neck.

We are both anxiously waiting the day we can have sex again. Dr. Rushing said we needed to wait at least six weeks. We do other things to alleviate the need, but I know he wants to bury himself in me as much as I want him. I wonder if we need to wait, surely the nanites will have fixed everything.

Lucy arrives home from school and is excited to find us in her kitchen. I've baked a cake and slice a sliver so she can taste it.

"Yummy!" She says laying down her fork and hugging me. "Mommy told me about your baby, Aunt Leslie. I feel really bad for you."

She reaches out and grabs Robbie as he walks up to her and messes her hair. "I'm sorry, Robbie. I know you were looking forward to being a dad."

"One day I'll be a dad." He says. "Until then I'll practice on you!" She laughs and he starts chasing her around the kitchen island. "Caught you!" He laughs tickling her.

I talk to Laura about finding a donor for a bone marrow transplant. If the chemo she is using now doesn't work, it is all medically they can do. "Thank God you're here! I don't know what I would do by myself. I wish Mom was here. She always knew how to take care of things. I mean the family always depended on her to guide us through these types of hard problems. It has been hard not having her around."

I look at Robbie who keeps his eyes on mine.

Our days continue one after another, until it is once again fall and Lucy's birthday. She is going to be nine and wants to invite all her friends to a swim party.

Robbie is back on tour for four months after the holidays, and then he is retiring from the band. The guys are upset, but understand. After the loss of his child and knowing that we don't want to be separated, they agree with his decision.

A week after Lucy's party, Laura is admitted to the hospital. They have found a marrow donor. She is hopeful, as are we. I have suffered too much loss; my first husband of thirty-five years through divorce and my precious baby Kara. It is time for a miracle; time for my darling Laura to have her miracle.

The day of the operation, Lucy goes to school as usual and we stay at the hospital with Preston and Tess, who decide they need to be here. We wait anxiously for the doctor, Preston pacing the floor in the family waiting room.

"I hate hospitals." Robbie says. "Mind if I go for a walk?"

I can see his agitation and I shake my head. "Go, get out of here and bring me back a Philly Cheese Steak or something really fattening."

The doctor finally appears by the double doors. Preston and I rise to meet him. "Everything went as it was supposed to. We will have to wait to see how she progresses. You can take her home in a month or so."

Preston is not coping with the strain of Laura's illness and it is showing in the way he keeps busy. "Can you stay with them for a few weeks?" His eyes plead. "Tess and I want to visit her family while we are here."

"Of course, you don't even need to ask." I reply giving him a hug. "Family sticks together."

"I really need help with Lucy. Laura usually takes care of everything." He complains.

Robbie is standing looking at us as we hug. I called him over and include him. "We are already taking care of things, Preston, so I don't know why you are even asking. It isn't like it's your only daughter facing death or anything."

I turn my back on him and walk away.

"Opal, you are the strong one in the family. You know I'm not good with this sort of thing." He wines with that puppy dog face he puts on. Tess is across the room and didn't hear him call me 'Opal'.

"You are really so pathetic! Such a coward! Go! Robbie and I will take care of Laura and Lucy like always. You're not here for me, but maybe your daughter would like to know her father cares for her and wants to be by her side."

I am so mad at this sniveling selfish man. We didn't need him, but maybe Laura does.

"Robbie and I will go home and meet Lucy's bus. You stay here until we get back."

I turn to Robbie. "Now, what is wrong with you? Why were you looking at me like that?"

"He was hugging you."

"Annd?" We had just talked to the doctor, and then he told me about the trip he wanted to take with Tess and asked if we could stay with Laura and Lucy."

"I don't know," he said. "He doesn't seem very fatherly."

"What do you mean?"

"I can't put my finger on it right now. Just don't really...." He rubbed his face. "Anyway, I found you a Philly Cheese thingy." He smirks.

"Oh goody! I'm starving!" I kiss him on the cheek. I take a deep breath and breathe in the smell of tantalizing fat."

"You don't usually eat meat. What's up?"

"Maybe it's the nanites." I pass the buck. I stuff my face

with half the sandwich. Robbie eats the rest.

After being in the hospital all day, I need a bath. I put in some bubbles and it is so hot, I have to add cold water to temper it. Robbie shows up to join me and we spend our time exploring possibilities of making each other happy. He eventually gets out and hands me a towel and we move to the bed to finish our adventures in pleasure.

After getting Lucy to the bus stop in the morning, I spend the day at the hospital with Laura. Robbie stays home and prepares dinner. He is a fare cook if the meal is simple. Lucy loves that he is there when she gets home from school. Then after dinner, he will bring her to the hospital to visit her mother.

Five weeks later, we bring Laura home from the hospital. She sleeps through the night. Now it is just a waiting game to see how the marrow transplant progresses. She looks like walking death.

I am really worried.

After summer and the beginning of a new school year in the fall, we are talking about Thanksgiving and the fast approaching Christmas holiday. Laura is looking better, but her white blood cell count is still elevated. The transplant isn't working and the atmosphere in the house is quickly becoming morose.

Preston returns from Florida, but his presence is like

fingernails on chalkboard.

Laura tries to lighten everyone's spirits by pretending she is fine. Lucy watches her mother's every move like she is expecting her to disappear. I finally get Preston alone and try to reason with him about how his attitude affects Laura. I keep uplifting music a constant in the house and it seems to help lift her spirits.

I believe in music to be healing and want to make sure the atmosphere is flooded with God's words, so I mainly play Christian music and light classical. Laura wants to start attending church on Sundays, so we all go with her. She looks happier.

After Thanksgiving, Laura takes a turn for the worse and the doctor admits her to the hospital. He asks if he can have a meeting with the family a few days later and tells us Laura is losing her battle and there is nothing more he can do. We take her home to watch over her ourselves. The only thing we can do is make her comfortable and let her know how much we love her.

Lucy understands her mother is dying and doesn't want to leave her bedside. Laura wants her to have a normal life and insists she return to school.

"How are you this morning?" I open the curtains in Laura's bedroom.

She looks at me and smiles. "Guess I feel a little better."

I reach across her bed to adjust the bedcovers, but feel a tug at my neck. The ruby heart pendant is in her hand and a strange look is on her face. She looks deep into my eyes. "Mom?"

I look down, but nod.

"Why?"

"Your dad didn't want you to know. He said you would hate me, and I couldn't stand that." Tears run down my cheeks and I wiped them away. I chance a look at her. "I wanted you to know, but I didn't want to cause you pain, or maybe your rejection would have caused me pain. So many times I wanted to tell you." I kiss her and run my hands over her cheeks.

"Anyway, your dad told me he fell in love with Tess and that he wanted to declare that I was dead. He insisted it would be better for everyone and as you know, I don't ever go against him. I'm afraid I insisted on coming back anyway. I thought if I pretended to be a long lost cousin, it could explain why I looked like myself and yet allow me to be near my family."

"Oh my God! Mommy!" She throws her arms around me and hugs me close. She hasn't called me Mommy since she was a little girl. "I have missed you so much! Thank God, you're alive!"

"Laura, I love you, my sweet baby girl!" I sniff. "I am so sorry I deceived you. Can you forgive me?"

"Oh, Mom! Of course I do. Boy Dad is going to have some explaining to do when I see him!" She laughs. "Oh no!" She looks sad.

"What?"

"Your baby was my little sister. I lost a little sister." A tear drops down her cheek.

I can only shake my head in affirmation.

"I'm so glad I know. Now I won't be worried about Lucy, since she will have you to look after her. I know she has her granddad, but he is practically useless when it comes to running a house or child rearing and Lucy doesn't really know Tess. I don't care if you want to tell her who you really are, or if you want to keep up the ruse, but I am so happy." She hugs me again. "She will have her grandmother and I will meet my baby sister in heaven."

"You know I will always take care of Lucy."

She starts giggling.

"What's so funny?"

"Robbie Brand is my stepfather. Cool! Do you think he would want to adopt me?"

She grins.

I shake my head at her antics. "Yeah, well think of this; I'm sixty-one and he is only half my age." I wiggle my eyebrows.

"You lecherous woman! He is very exciting, isn't he?"

"I love him, Laura. He makes me very happy and I know he loves me, too."

"I see the way he looks at you, Mom. I know he loves you and I am so glad you have each other." Suddenly, she looks very sad. "I just worry about Lucy. I will leave it up to you whether you tell her who you really are or not."

"As long as I have breath, I will never let anything happen to her, Laura. You know that!" I watch my daughter. She is very weak and her skin looks grey. I kiss her cheek and tell her to rest.

"I am very tired, but so thankful. I think I will rest." She closes her eyes and never opens them again and dies a few days later.

We bury Laura a week before Christmas. I've lost my two daughters. I lost my life, although I regained a new one. They have caused deep emotional pains and great joys. The only good thing I got out of my new life was Robbie. But all of this is nothing compared to what Lucy is going through. She lost her mother. I will be there for her.

After the funeral, Robbie takes me in his arms, and with such tenderness, he makes love to me. It felt like heaven to have him take my mind off my loss. I am a bit louder than I should be as he ravishes me, but he uses his kisses to muffle the sound of my desire.

Preston and Tess left right after the funeral and I don't

expect that I'll see them again in this life. Preston seemed happy to hear that Robbie and I are going to adopt Lucy. "She will be with her grandmother. That will mean a lot to her, if you decide to tell her.

I will make sure she has the funds for college and send you the information. Let me know what she needs and I will help." He kisses my cheek. "I'm a very old man now, Opal. We have been a big part of each other's lives for a long time. Thank you for being there for our girls. I love you." He actually has tears in his eyes.

CHAPTER 22

Three years later

After Robbie retired from the band, we bought a coffee shop and have thrived doing something we love. He visits Guatemala every few months and of course our coffee comes from the farm. We spend most of Lucy's eleventh summer on the farm. She enjoys herself, but misses her friends.

Now she is turning twelve and she wants to spend the day at the mall, shopping and eating out. I am fastening my seat belt when I notice her staring at me. "What's wrong?"

"You never seem to age. You are just a pretty as when I first met you. We must have some really good genes." She smiles. "I hope I'm as beautiful as you one day."

"Please," I laugh. "I have to work hard to keep from aging. You are the one who is beautiful!"

We are travelling east on I-24 when I hear a loud crunching sound and see a semi jerk to the right and jackknife. The trailer it is pulling screeches as it lands on its side on the pavement and lashes out like the arm of a pinball machine, slamming into an SUV, sending it flying across the median, and into our lane of traffic.

Lucy screams and I turn the wheel trying to avoid the collision, but there isn't enough space in front of the car to maneuver. The SUV crashes into the front of our car and sends us careening sideways over the shoulder of the road and through the guardrail. All I can see is white from the air bags, until long metal strips strike through them scattering plastic and dust and enter our chests. Suddenly, we are heading into the trees, which stop our car instantly with a shuddering crash.

I look at Lucy hanging sideways in her seat belt. One of the metal strips is stabbing her chest.

"Lucy!" I shake her, but there isn't any response. I can tell she is breathing, because blood is lightly spraying out her nose with each breath.

I push the metal strip out of my own chest and gasp when I see the hole it made. I release Lucy's seat belt and check her for lacerations. She has a lot of blood pooling on her blouse and when I open it there is a hole in her chest the size of a quarter.

I start crying. I just can't lose someone else, especially not Lucy. I drag her to myself and hold her close to the cut on my own chest and give the nanites instructions to leave me and heal her. They let me know they understand. I know we will be healed before we get to the hospital. After about ten minutes, she stirs and moans.

"Lucy." I turn her face to me. "Lucy." I say, urgently. "Open your eyes, sweetie. We've been in an accident. You're going to be alright, baby girl."

She looks at me. "What is happening?"

"We were in an accident. A car on the other side of the road came across the median and hit us. Let's get out of the car. Can you move?"

"My door won't open!" She starts panicking.

"Can you crawl towards me?" I hold out my arms to help her out my side of the car. I reach in the glove box and pop the trunk, taking out a blanket and wrapping it around us. I check her chest and see that the wound is still bloody, but healing. I carry her backpack and grab the first aid kit.

We sit away from the car and I start cleaning up the blood. Lucy stares at the car. "Gosh, Aunt Leslie the car is wrecked!"

"Yeah, I'm afraid it is a total loss, but at least we have our lives. How do you feel?"

"I have some pain in my right knee and of course my chest hurts some. I think there is some glass in my forehead."

"We will have to go to the hospital and get checked out."

She frowns. "I don't like hospitals they smell like

antiseptic and alcohol. They remind me of Mommy. She starts to cry."

"They won't keep us. Just want to make sure everything is alright." I reassure her.

There are sirens and bright flashing lights arriving at the scene of the accident. While we wait, the sun goes down. It is very cold and we can see our breath in the LED lantern I retrieved from the trunk.

We watch the lights from the highway and hear shouting as police, ambulances, and fire trucks arrive. After some time, we can see the glow of flashlights heading our way.

"Wow! I can't believe we survived that!" Lucy is taking it all in stride.

"I'm going to call Robbie." I dig in my purse for my cell. "Robbie, we've been in an accident. Both Lucy and I are alright, but we are going to the hospital to get checked out." I continue my explanation of the wreck and ring off as the police approach.

They help us to the road and instead of an ambulance, put us in the back of the police cruiser and take us to the hospital. They are astonished that we survived with so little damage. The people in the SUV weren't so lucky.

Robbie is soon holding my hand and covering me with kisses. "You scared me!"

"Lucy?"

"She is going to be fine, Opal. She just has some minor lacerations and bruising. All in all, you both fared well. The car, not so much."

He leans in and deepens his kiss and then smiles.

"This was a real accident, you know."

He looks off in the distance as if concentrating on something. "I just wish we could be sure."

"Whaat? Now how can an accident like that be orchestrated? I didn't know you are such a conspiracy theorist!" I smirk.

"You are right, nothing has happened in years, but I'm still on my guard."

"Everything looks alright." A young doctor signs a release form. "I think the police want to speak with you." He motions to the hallway.

"What about Lucy? Can she go home?"

"She is getting an x-ray on her knee. Then she can go home." He leaves the room.

"If they just leave her alone, the nanites will fix her." I whisper.

Robbie turns quickly. "What?"

"I was talking to myself." I smile.

"How will the nanites fix her? What did you do?" He is frowning. I watch his expression. He grabs my arm and shakes it. "What did you do?"

"Robbie, she had a long metal strip embedded in her chest. I couldn't let her die. So I yanked her to my own wound and told the nanites to heal her." I look at him desperately. "I can't lose her too!"

He shakes his head. "Those nanites aren't configured to work with her DNA. We don't know what will happen."

"I am willing to take that chance to save her." My eyes plead with him to understand. "I wasn't going to let her die or bleed to death before my eyes. I just couldn't. Oh, Robbie she has to be okay." The tears run down my face.

"Shhh. It's okay Opal. Calm down. We'll just have to trust everything will be all right. After all, they have healed her."

He knew I was about to lose it and he didn't want to deal with me in the crazy mental state I was in when Kara died. He strokes my hair and kisses my cheek. "It will be okay, baby." He takes me in his arms and holds me. "Are you going to be okay to speak to the police?"

I nod and he tucks me close to his side and walks me to the waiting cop. By the time I finish explaining what happened at the accident, Lucy is ready to go home. There aren't any scars on Lucy or myself. It is as if the accident never happened. I worry that the nanites might cause her some problems, but it seems I worried for naught for she is happy and healthy.

We fall into an easy daily pattern that flows smoothly for all four of us. Preston stays away. I am sure he is glad to be free of responsibilities. Lucy continues her schooling, and Robbie and I run the coffee shop.

We adopt Lucy, but she wants to keep her father's last name in remembrance of him. Therefore, she will remain Lucille Jean March. Even though the adoption is final, she still calls us by our first names, Leslie and Robbie.

We hire two part-time workers to help at the shop; one for the morning and one for the evening. This gives us an opportunity to go across the street to the apartment and spend some quality time together in bed. We both feel a bit hampered making love with Lucy's bedroom next to ours. We can't figure out why we aren't pregnant anymore. We both want to try for a baby again.

Robbie starts kissing me before he opens the door. He drops his jacket on the floor and reaches over to sweep mine off my shoulders. His mouth presses hungrily on my lips, while his tongue invades my mouth and tastes me. We both groan starved for each other. I unbutton my blouse as he reaches around my back and quickly unhooks my bra. My blouse on the floor, I drop my arms and let him push my bra off, while my hands undo his shirt buttons. He draws my breast to his mouth and his tongue nips and licks my nipples and then he sucks until my core pulses with desire. We both make quick work of our boots and jeans and his hands slips under my lace panties and between my thighs. Oh, the man can do wondrous things with his hands. I whimper. He nips me in the tender area under my ear and makes a trail of kisses down my neck.

He picks me up, walks back to the bedroom and lays me on the bed. He pulls off my panties and lies beside me running his hands all over my body. "You are so beautiful, wife." I stroke him, but he pushes my hand away. "You do that and this will be a very short love making session." Finally his hand grasps my hair and pulls my face back to his as he devours my mouth. He growls and slips between my legs, he enters me, as my legs slip around his waist. "You are so wet and warm and tight." He speaks against my lips. I can feel him pulsing within as he waits to calm down.

"Please, please, Robbie..."

"Um. Begging, I like that!" He chuckles.

When we are both sated, we snuggle further in the covers and talk about losing our daughters. I still receive messages from the nanites occasionally, asking about Kara. Maybe we will get pregnant again. Robbie wants to be a father, so I plan on working at it. This is a very enjoyable endeavor.

"Umm." I turn to him, stroke the black hair on his muscular chest, following its progression to his six-pack-abs, and further. Before I can get to his groin, he is standing at attention and ready to make me a happy woman.

Our days are happy ones. We work, play, make mad love, and watch over Lucy. She is turning thirteen in a few months and we want to take a trip to the coffee farm. Robbie is hiring a manager for the coffee shop and we decide to sell the apartment. I save my Subaru for Lucy and we'll buy a new pickup when we return from Guatemala. Besides, my man looks good on his new Harley, but I think he would look even better driving a pickup.

Robbie must have fallen off the radar, since people don't recognize him anymore. Of course it could be the "stash" and the soul patch, which I am 'digging'. He cuts his hair shorter and gets another tattoo with Kara's name. It is a small stork carrying a baby with her name entwined over his heart. It is so sweet and so like him. He has a real bad boy look that I adore. I get a sparkly belly ring that he finds exciting and although he likes my long curly locks, I keep it cut to the middle of my back. It makes life much easier.

There's been no sign of Zoe. I wonder if she returned to the clinic. I still can't believe she left Lonnie.

CHAPTER 23

Lucy starts dating and Robbie insists on interviewing her dates. She just rolls her eyes at him, but he is so damn irresistible, she lets him without much resistance. Her dates are young and only want to go bowling or skating. I think she is too young to date, but she seems to be a fairly good judge of character, that we trust her choices. Her boyfriends are more interested in playing video games than kissing.

Robbie is a remarkable man; tender, kind, gentle, fun, considerate, and all mine. Well, I share him with Lucy. He is her substitute father figure and friend.

Lucy never gets sick. She did break her finger once, but it healed on its own, which means the nanites are on the job. She complained a few times that she has headaches, but nothing beyond that. I don't know if the nanites are developing neural pathways like they have in me or if they aren't as advanced as mine, because Lucy's DNA is different from my own. We are still unaware of the consequences of their involvement in her physiology. It is a worry I live with daily.

Robbie provides Lucy with a horse of her own on the farm. She names him Thaddeus. He is a black beauty and she rides him daily throughout the farm. Everyone on the coffee plantation loves Lucy and she can charm the scales off a snake. Garrett is totally enamored with her, which seems to lessen his hostility towards me, since he thinks she is my niece. Lucy calls him Uncle Gary and he lets her.

Stephanie adores her too, and is constantly ordering clothes, DVDs, and jewelry for her online. They take her one afternoon to Tikal to see the Mayan Ruins and keep her busy visiting all the many villages in Guatemala. We all take a few days and visit the beach where Robbie and I met.

We are celebrating our seventh anniversary and inviting all our friends to an open house celebration. Robbie wants to renew our vows so he is ramping up security. He is still concerned for my safety.

Stephanie, Lucy, and I go shopping for special dresses in Guatemala City. She knows several dressmakers and we show them what kind of dresses we like. Since I am getting remarried, I chose a long silky off white lace bustier dress with diaphanous layers of pale lavender silk reaching to the floor. The silk flows like liquid and when I walk it looks like I am floating.

"Oh my God!" Lucy's jaw drops. "That is so gorgeous, Aunt Leslie. You definitely have to get that one." She plays with the lavender layers. "The color looks good with your hair, too."

"She's right!" Stephanie exclaims. "This is the perfect dress for you. Can't wait to see Robbie's face when he sees you in this."

I look in the mirrors. It is beautiful. "You sure it doesn't look like lingerie?"

"What? No! It's perfect!" Lucy is adamant.

I smile. I really did like it. It is the most beautiful dress I have ever seen. Delicate, like a little rain and it will melt. "Okay, I choose this one."

"Shoes?"

"No. Barefoot."

I am shocked. "Barefoot, Lucy? I can't go barefoot. There are rocks and plants with thorns."

She put her finger to her pursed lips thinking. "Okay then, thong sandals with teeny tiny straps, so it looks like you're barefoot."

Stephanie is shaking her head no. "I think you should buy these." She holds up a pair of stilettos that look like they are made of glass. Next to the dress, they too look urethral and in a prismatic way takes on the lavender hue."

Lucy and I both oo and aw. And that was it.

We go to a nearby spa and have the works; nails, hair, facials, and makeup. Lucy wants to have her hair died in "ombre" fashion with the lighter color on the bottom. She also asks for a tattoo of her mother's name in a heart on her ankle. I didn't want to agree, but as she insists, I finally gave in and tell her she can have it done in henna. It isn't permanent, but I don't want to allow her to have a real tattoo until I talk with Robbie. Although he has several tattoos that are so sexy on him, they make him look like a badass.

Stephanie walks up to me. "Bet you're thinking about Robbie."

"What?" I grin. "How did you know?"

"I've seen that look on you a million times."

I sigh. "God, I love that man!"

She laughs. "Me too."

Our Anniversary party is lovely. Robbie is dressed in off white tuxedo pants with a matching shirt and a lavender silk cummerbund that matches my dress perfectly. The top buttons to his shirt are unbuttoned and he doesn't wear a tie. He looks so handsome I can't stop looking at him. I walk down the stairs and feel our familiar hum. He finds me and envelopes me in his arms. His hair has gotten longer and he hasn't cut it. I reach over and brush it back from his forehead as he stares into my eyes. We don't need to talk; we communicate in silence our need for one another.

"You are so beautiful he says before he kisses me." That kiss goes straight to every nerve ending in my body and resides as an ache in my heart. I will never get enough of his essence. I moan my satisfaction. "Please don't do that," he chuckles, "unless you want me to make love you in front of all of our guests."

I smile with my eyes and moan again.

He grins. "Shall we proceed?" He motions for me to join him in front of the audience and he begins his vows.

"My darling wife. I promise to love you; and I have and always will. I promise to protect you; and I have and always will. I promise to love you in sickness and health; and I have and always will. I promise to be faithful to only you; and I have and always will. When my heart beats, it beats for you and always will. You take my breath away. When you are in my arms I have everything I will ever need to exist." He kisses my fingers. "I love you."

"Husband, I am complete when I look into your eyes, when I enter your presence, when I hear your voice, when I smell your essence, and when I feel your touch. You have made me want to be a better person, want to believe in goodness, want to reach a higher plateau of faith, try to be more just, try to see more goodness in others, and try to love more purely. Because of your love, I am part of something bigger, grander, more encompassing, more thrilling, and more expansive. I am loved by you and in love with you, Robbie."

He reaches in his pants pocket and pulls out a ring,

placing it on the middle finger of my right hand. "I promise you all of me." Then he kisses the ring on my finger. The ring is platinum with writing on it. *Tha gaol agam ort. Is thu m'annsachd* (I love you. Thou art my most beloved).

I reach out, take a necklace from Lucy, and place it around his neck. It is a flat disc made from white gold with a design like his Celtic tattoo, which circles his bicep. Lucy's, Kara's, my name, and room for more, are entwined in the design.

My only hope is that Lucy hasn't realized my real name was inscribed instead of Leslie's. Just as we kiss and the crowd moves, stands, and claps to congratulate us, a shot rings out and I take a hit in the head. Robbie drops with me to the ground.

"Opal!"

"I'm okay, Robbie. Someone is a bad shot. It's only grazed me." My hand comes away bloody and when I see it I faint for a seond.

There is pandemonium, but Robbie keeps me down and moves me quickly to the house. "Where are the damn guards I hired?" I hear him as I awaken.

I look towards the balcony and see Zoe staring at me through a door that was left standing open. Robbie leans forward and shuts it, blocking out my view. He speaks into a walkie-talkie.

"Please, find Lucy and bring her to the house. Protect her with your life!"

A few minutes later Lucy is brought in the house surrounded by two guards. She drops to the floor beside me.

"Thank God! I knew you were hit and I saw who did it! There was a woman standing on the balcony. I think I have seen her before." She speaks quickly and breathlessly.

I take her hand. "I saw her too when I woke up."

"Who?" Robbie asks.

"Zoe. I saw Zoe standing on the balcony before you shut the door. She was looking at me like she was angry."

He leans in and kisses me on the forehead. He has a wet washcloth in his hand and he swipes at the blood staining my hair. "Shit, it's already healed." He remembers and looks at Lucy and cringes.

Several hours later and the guests are gone and the police are still looking for Zoe.

"Do you suppose she could have been the one to sabotage the zip-line?"

He stares at me soberly. "How would she know we were going to take the zip-line when we did? That's what baffles me. Only you, I, and Stephanie knew before hand."

"Whatever is happening, that woman is definitely involved. We have to find her."

"We? Just let the police handle it, Robbie."

Lucy is sitting quietly in the recliner watching us. She finally sits up and gets our attention. "Who is Opal?"

We both stare at her. She points to Robbie.

"Your new necklace has the name Opal on it. Do you have a little girl named Opal? Like my grandmother?"

Robbie and I look at each other. I sigh. "Lucy, I am your grandmother. It's a very long involved story and if you want to hear it, you shall, but can it wait until later?"

"You are my grandmother? You're too young to be my grandmother. Who is Leslie?"

"I am both Opal and Leslie and as I said before, I will tell you the whole story later. Right now we have to feed all these people, because they all have to be interviewed by the police."

People help themselves from the buffet tables and we open the coffee bar as well. The police are very methodical in their approach to speaking with every person who in attendance at the anniversary party, except there is no clue where Zoe went. It is very late when everyone finally leaves.

"Are you hungry? I can order something from the kitchen. We never had any cake and there is still so much food left from the "almost" party."

She nods her head. "Let's eat. I don't want to think about this stuff anymore. You were shot at by a crazy woman!" Lucy says.

"I'm sure they will catch her."

Robbie rubs his face and makes a phone call to the kitchen to order food.

We sit at the kitchen table and I explain to Lucy about the deception. I tell her that Laura knew before she died, that I was her mother and not her cousin. Lucy seems to take it all in stride and immediately starts calling me grandma.

It is late and we finally go to our rooms. Robbie makes sure to lock the windows and shut the curtains. Then he reaches for me and kisses my neck. "I didn't get to tell you how beautiful you look."

"Yes, it is a lovely dress."

"The dress is only beautiful because you are wearing it."

Robbie continues to nibble along my neck, kissing my jaw and finally reaching my lips. He kisses my top lip and then kisses my bottom lip, letting his tongue run lightly around them. I open my mouth in invitation when his tongue enters; the taste of him explodes my senses. We both moan and then he moves the tiny straps to my gown and deposits a row of kisses along the top of my breasts. Slowly, he unzips the gown letting his fingers run a trail down my spine setting off a line of hot sparks that cause me to quiver, as my gown slips to the floor in a silken pool. I am standing naked in a pair of crystal stilettoes. He gasps and his brows arch.

"I didn't want any panty lines."

He grins as his hand cups my breast and he flicks his thumb across my nipple. The one small action sends desire shooting through my body and I moan. Reaching up I begin unbuttoning his shirt and see the necklace lying on his chest.

"You are so damn sexy."

He takes off his shoes and drops his pants. I reach out and stroke him. It doesn't take long until we experience that connection that takes us beyond and back. I'm still shuddering when he pulls up the covers and we fall asleep holding each other. Tonight, we have this; our love. Tomorrow will bring its own set of rules.

༺ ༺ ༺ ༺ ༺

The day after the 'almost' party, I walk behind Stephanie's house to speak with her, but hear cursing and shouting. I see Garrett pacing on the patio talking on the phone. I don't mean to snoop, but I thought I heard my name.

"Yeah, you shot her. NOT! What was that Zoe? I should have killed her in the first place instead of leaving it up to you! This is getting out of hand! She had a child for Christ sake! We don't want to wait around until something happens that we can't control! It has to be taken care of now! Dammit, I'll do it! This is the problem with Sylvia's experiments; someone always has to exterminate them! Yeah, but Robbie doesn't know....."

He walks back in the house and I can't hear anymore.

My God! Garrett has been trying to kill me? Zoe? What if Stephanie is in on it? I need to tell Robbie. And what is it that Robbie doesn't know? I told him all about me. Did they kill my baby? I quickly make my way to the barn. "Robbie!"

He appears in an instant. "Opal?"

My arms are around him instantly and I bury my head against his chest. Tears threaten to fall, but I am too choked to talk.

"Shit! Opal. Come on baby. Come into the office. Sit here." He pushes me into a chair and falls to his knees his arms around me.

"We need to find Lucy. Where is Titan?" I start to panic. "Oh my God. Oh my God."

"Titan! Go find Lucy and bring her to the office in the stable." Robbie yells into a phone.

"Opal what's happened? Baby, you're scaring me."

I swallow and almost heave. I think I'm going to be sick. "I heard Garret talking on the phone to Zoe. They were talking about shooting me. He said *he* would kill me and that *he* always has to exterminate Sylvia's experiments. Then he said they didn't want to wait around until something happens they can't control. He was talking about our child. Do you think he killed her?"

Robbie is stunned. "No, you must have misunderstood. Not Garrett. He and Stephanie have been with me forever."

"That was another thing he said...Robbie doesn't know." I can tell he is turning this information over in his mind. "Garrett would have known we were going zip-lining. Zoe could have easily committed all the vandalism. I know she was in Nashville. Hell, she shot me at the party."

Titan walks in with Lucy in tow. "What's going on?" she asks.

"We have to get out of here. We'll go back to Nashville. Call the airfield and get us a helicopter and a chartered flight to the US. We have to pack."

I take Lucy to the bathroom, while Robbie brings Titan up to date with what I heard.

When we come back, Titan nods his head at me to let me know he understands our position. Robbie asks Stephanie to come to the barn. He tells her and she falls to the floor crying. He asks her to come with us and she agrees.

"We can leave tomorrow morning, Robbie. Garrett will be leaving for a meeting with coffee buyers in Japan." She says.

"Should we wait that long?" I ask.

"He's waited this long. Besides I think if Zoe wanted to kill you she would have by now. She may be to blame for all the vandalism, but I don't believe she will kill you." Stephanie says.

"You aren't going to say anything to him, are you?" I turn her to face me. "He's your husband. How do we know you aren't acting with him?"

"Because Robbie is like my own son. I would never put him in danger. I love him. He's the only family I have left." She reaches out to him. "You know that, don't you?"

He goes into her arms. "I trust you, Stephanie. We have been together off and on for thirty years; ever since I was a teen. As far as I am concerned, you are my mother."

Robbie holds out his arm and I go to him as he hugs me. "You can trust her, Opal."

"Thirty years? Since you were a teen? Oh God, you're a HuMEM."

He stares at me like I've lost my mind. "Think about it, Robbie. That's why you are never sick. Not even a sniffle in the entire time I've known you. And...you don't even realize you're a HuMEM."

He turns to Stephanie. "Steph?"

I grab his arms and shake him a little. "This makes even more sense. That's why we hum. Why you don't age, but all the guys in the band look so much older than you. This is great!"

I'm crying tears of joy streaming down my face. "I won't lose you!"

Robbie has no expression on his face. "Stephanie? Why?"

She clears her throat and speaks slowly . "There were... extenuating circumstances. I can't tell you everything, because

I don't know everything. But, yes, you are a HuMEM."

"Why can't I remember?" Robbie rubs his face.

"We need to concentrate on getting away from here, sir." Titan says, stepping back into the office and bringing us back to the present problem. "We should all stay together tonight. Ma'am," he nods at Stephanie. "You can get your things in the morning."

"What excuse do I give Garrett for not sleeping in his bed?"

"I am sick and need your help. I hit my head and might have a concussion and you have to stay up with me," I say quickly.

"You're a HuMEM and he knows it. Won't work."

"We're having a movie marathon." Lucy offers.

"Fine. Let's go pack." I say.

CHAPTER 24

Lucy has been having headaches and when we return to Nashville, they get worse. The doctor thinks it is stress from losing her mother, the accident, and school. We change our diet a bit, thinking maybe she has food allergies. We try a wheat-free diet for several months to no avail. I think we all feel better, but the headaches only get worse. We think maybe it's mold, so we have a house inspector examine the house. He doesn't find anything.

Stephanie is living with us. She said she feels bad running out on Garrett, but she did suspect he was doing some pretty horrible things for Dr. Rushing. She didn't realize it was murder. She is a big help with Lucy and the coffee shop.

The security around us is beefed up. Garrett understands we know he is involved with trying to kill me. Stephanie told him after we arrived back in Nashville. Guess he thinks his cover is blown, since we don't see he or Zoe hanging around.

Robbie accepts his HuMEM status, but isn't happy that he can't remember. He is leaving for California to a recording studio. He is asked by the band to help them with a new album. He told them he would help, but no tours. Stephanie travels with him, so my days are very busy and Lucy has to take care of herself. She is now thirteen and old enough to handle getting her own dinner. Her headaches nearly disappear for a while and she's in a happier mood and seems content. But when Robbie returns the headaches do too.

"I don't think Lucy is allergic to you, darling." He is convinced she is only sick when he is around. "After all, you weren't around when we went shopping and she had such a headache so strong she couldn't do anything but run into the women's bathroom and lock herself in. She wouldn't come out for a while."

"You don't suppose the nanites have tried to create neural pathways in her like they did you? Remember what happened when Kara's frequency changed and you suffered so much pain when you were around me? Could it be something like that?"

I look at him, but can't respond. I am frightened that that is exactly what is happening to her. "No. We can't think like that! Surely it isn't."

He walks to the kitchen and back. "We have to take her to Dr. Rushing. She needs to examine her."

"No! I won't allow it!" Tears sprang to my eyes and threatened to flood down my face. "That woman is a menace.

You have to promise me Robbie that you will stay away from that place. Dr. Rushing is a self-serving lunatic! I'm certain she had something to do with Kara's death."

"Opal, you owe it to Lucy to eliminate the possibility of interference by the nanites. You must see that?"

"No, no, no. Never again will we step foot in that place."

He sat down next to me on the couch. "Maybe in some way, we have all gone 'whacko' after being in that clinic and at the hands of that crazy woman. And I want some answers. I want to find out about my past." He puts his arms around me. "Okay. We'll see what happens. We don't have to do anything right away. I'm just concerned for Lucy."

I lean in and kiss him. "You are such a wonderful man! Do you know that? So absolutely adorable! Sexy! Handsome! Intelligent! Did I mention sexy?"

His hands pull me onto his lap and wrap around me bringing me close. I lay my head on his chest and listen to his heartbeat. Rubbing my hand over his pecks the rhythm picks up and I feel his erection.

He smiles. "I am totally weak where you are concerned; putty in your hands. One touch and I'm on fire."

Our days flow swiftly, but I see less and less of Lucy. She makes excuses to sleep at a friend's house or go to bed early. We have a kind of dance we do when we are both home together. She enters one room and I exit. She doesn't mind being around Robbie or Stephanie, so I let them be. Finally, I think it is time to confront the issue.

"Lucy," she gets up to leave, "please, dearest, let's talk." "I'm not mad at you grandma; it just hurts to be in the same room with you." She grasps her head. "Please, just write me an email or a letter. Oh God, it hurts."

I nod and we look at each other over the distance of the front door and the kitchen sink where I lean with great sadness. "I love you."

I decide to write her an email.

Lucy, do you remember when we were in the car accident? You were mortally injured and I didn't think you were going to live, which was more than I could stand. I asked nanites to leave me and enter you to heal you, so you would survive. I think this is where the problem lies.

In me, the nanites have created neural pathways and I have the ability to communicate with them. Since the ones in you have come from me, I can only surmise they are trying to do the same to you. Please, try to communicate with them.

One problem I faced with Kara during her gestation was an imbalance in frequency. She and I were always in sync, but I experienced severe pain all over my body when I was around Robbie. The baby's frequency was in flux and shifted several times during pregnancy. Perhaps, this is what is happening between us.

The nanites were also mixed with my DNA, which could be another reason for the pain you are experiencing. As I noted before, we can only guess as to the reason you experience pain around me.

I love you and hope you find you can communicate with them. I await your response. If you want, you may speak with Robbie about this.

Grandma

That evening, Robbie tells me that Lucy asked to speak with him. I show him the email so he won't be blindsided and maybe try to be ready for the onslaught of questions I am sure Lucy will ask.

When she comes home from school, they get on his motorcycle and drive away. I go to the coffee shop (DOUGH JOE—a play on the word dojo) to grab the receipts and miscellaneous papers the accountant needs. We are going to enlarge the coffee shop by acquiring the shop next door.

When I get back home, Robbie and Lucy are home as well. "Please, don't get up, I'll make myself scarce." I quickly go to the sanctuary of the den.

Robbie comes in a few minutes later. He sighs. "Lucy isn't very happy to know that you did this to her, but she understands that you had no option; you couldn't let her die and she said she would have done the same for you."

He pulls me close when the tears start running down

my cheeks. "Baby, it's alright. She's a remarkable young woman, you know."

I nod.

"She is going to try to communicate with them. She let it be known that she thinks she sees things once in a while. The nanites ask her about Kara."

I pull back and look at his face. "Kara, are you sure?"

"Yea, they ask her the same way they ask you." He kisses my forehead then rubs the back of my neck. "They must have created the neural pathways. She also said…and I don't want you to panic, but she said she feels as if she is unable to control her urges to strike out at you when she is near you. She said she is in so much pain it is like becoming unglued. She just wants to stop the pain."

My hands cover my mouth. "What are we going to do? I can't live without her in my life. I am all she has, Robbie."

"I know, love. I know." He pulls me close and runs his hands over my hair. "We'll think of something. We need to give her time to communicate with them, if she can."

"Do you "hum" with her? Like how we hum?"

"No. That only happens with you, love." He covers my mouth with his in a tender kiss. "You're my other half."

Another week passes and the accountant has let us know our bid is accepted for the shop. The DOUGH JOE is now closed for expansion and Robbie's new job is being there for

Lucy. He finally receives a call from Garrett. There are some matters to take care of at the coffee farm. Stephanie travels with him.

I receive an email from Lucy.

Grandma, I have successfully communicated with the nanties about the frequency. They said they would change it. Don't know how long it will take, but let's try every day to see how it's going. Lucy.

It takes three days before we are able to stand next to each other without Lucy feeling pain. We are so happy. She hugs me and hangs on for dear life. We spend every moment we can together and wait anxiously for Robbie to return.

Lucy wants it to be a surprise, so we wait together with our arms around each other as he exits the plane and moves through the gate and into our arms. He is smiling and kissing both of us.

"I see something wonderful has happened! I love my bionic girls."

"New song?" I tease.

His smile widens. "Actually, it is. Let's get some lunch."

I know he will share, but don't want to press him for more at this time. Lucy and I still have our arms around each other when a rogue cart comes careening our way. We jump apart just in time to keep it from hitting us. I think to grab Robbie by the jacket and yank him with me, but it clips his right heel.

"What the hell?" He falls to the floor and grabs his ankle. Then all pandemonium breaks out. The cart continues out the sliding glass doors and crashes into a waiting minibus full of travelers.

Several airport guards chase after the cart and I look around trying to find where the cart came from. I spot a familiar face in the distant crowd standing around the luggage carousel, but I'm distracted trying to help Robbie up—when I look back, Zoe is gone.

"That's an electric cart. They don't run by themselves." Robbie limps to the nearest bench.

"Unless they are rigged." I counter. "I saw Zoe over by the luggage carousel."

He looks confused. "What does that woman want? Did you two have a fight or something?"

"No. That's just it. No fight. She was very protective of me when I was at the clinic. We had a few disagreements, but they were about keeping me safe...nothing else."

I reach out for Lucy. She hugs me. "Are you okay grandma?"

"I'm fine, darling." She leans her head on my shoulder. "You okay?" She nods.

We give our stories to the police and then we are permitted to leave.

"Do you need to go to the doctor, Robbie?"

"No," he says. "All better now." He walks without any trouble.

"HuMem." I tease as he frowns.

Several days later, the investigation at the airport is complete. The authorities decide that it was a prank or maybe a gang initiation. No one was hurt and there wasn't anything that showed up on the security tapes. They therefore consider the incident closed and in no way connected to any of the other attempts on our lives.

Two weeks later and Lucy's frequency is off. She is keeping her distance from me and spending all her time with Robbie. We take a plane to New York, do some sightseeing, and buy some new clothes. They sit in First Class and I sit as far back as I can in coach.

I am shopping one day when I run into Zoe in Macys. "What are you doing Zoe?" I tugged at her arm. "I can't believe you are trying to kill me."

She huffs at me. "I'm not trying to kill you, Opal! Damn! You need to find a place where you can hide. Others want to kill you."

"Yeah, that crazy Dr. Rushing and her protégé, Garrett?"

"You know about Garrett? We can't be seen together. I'll try to get in touch with you another way. Use burner phones so you can throw them away." She hands me a small card with list of phone numbers. "One of these will work."

"What is going on?" I yell as I see her retreating down an aisle. "Shit!" I stomp my foot. What the bloody hell is going on? I pick up my bags and head for the main floor. I need to get back and tell Robby. I am in our room taking a nap when a boisterous Lucy dances her way through the house. Robbie finds me in our room and throws himself on the bed.

"I'm exhausted!" He kicks off his shoes and curls himself around my back, draping his arms around me. "You okay?"

"I talked to Zoe today. She said she isn't trying to kill me, but others are." I sniff. Now that he is here holding me, I let all my emotions surface. "She says we should use a burner phone to contact her."

"She is the only one we ever see. We can't trust her. She may be lying to you. How does she show up wherever we go? Something isn't adding up, Opal."

"I don't know, she told me to find a place to hide. She seems sincerely worried for us."

Lucy is able with the nanites help to alter her frequency again. Life goes back to normal.

We are heading to a log cabin retreat in Sapphire, NC for a "hidden" sabbatical. The mountains are beautiful. The mornings are foggy and the days are sunny. The evenings are still cool and I love the smell of the pines, wood smoke, and raw earth. The aroma is life; very intoxicating.

Lucy goes for morning walks with Robbie and he stomps around with me during the day. We don't see another soul as long as we stay up in the cabin. One morning, Lucy isn't feeling well and Robbie decides we need supplies. He takes the car to the nearest grocery store and Lucy stays with me.

I am in the small kitchen making coffee when something slams into my back. I turn in time to see Lucy get up and grab a knife from the counter.

"Lucy! What are you doing?"

Her eyes are glazed and her hair looks like it is windswept, but not in a good way. She has her mouth open and is drooling. She holds the knife with two hands over her head stabs me with it. I am too shocked to do anything.

"You killed me!" She screams. "You let those monstrous things in me and they are killing me. No! You are killing me!" The she screams repeatedly. "Make it stop! Make it stop!"

"Lucy! Please!" I beg her. My hand comes away from my side covered in blood. I'm not worried for myself. I am a HuMEM. I will heal.

"No, I can't stand the pain! You have to die! Then I'll have peace! You have to die!" She tries to plunge the knife repeatedly wherever she can.

I can't run. I know this isn't Lucy's fault. She can't be blamed for her actions. I did this to her, by asking the nanites to heal her. I pick up the phone and press speed dial.

"Help me!" Lucy slides down to the floor, setting on the red throw rug. No, it isn't a rug. It is my blood.

"I'm sorry, Lucy. I love you!" I whisper.

Zoe suddenly appears in the kitchen and takes in the situation. "How are you?"

"Bleeding, but I'll live."

Zoe takes out a hypodermic. "With your permission, I'll put her out for a while."

I nod.

"Robbie will be back. Guess I'll have to bite the bullet and take her to the clinic." I blow out my breath. "Wish there is an option B."

"You shouldn't have done that to the kid. I understand you felt you had no other way to keep her alive, but this is what happens when we mess with Mother Nature."

"Zoe, thanks."

"Life sucks!" She says.

"Did you really leave Lonnie?"

"I'm not here for confession. You healed yet?" She leans me forward and pulls up my sweater examining the wounds. "Yep looks good. It's closed. You'll probably still be sore for a few days. The wounds don't look very deep." She searches the cabin. "Where's Robbie?"

"He went to the market for food. How do you know

Robbie? It was you doing all those things, right?"

"I told you, I'm not here for confession."

She picks up Lucy and lays her on the couch.

"Go get cleaned up and clean up the kid. We have to be ready to go when Robbie gets back. I've called in a few favors and we can leave for Switzerland in a few hours."

She crosses her arms over her chest. "What do you think is going on here, Opal?"

"I'm confused. Ever since I entered your world at the clinic my life has been so confusing."

"It's all about you. It would have been okay if you had developed into a normal HuMEM, but when the nanites chose you to be a worthy candidate for their attempts to become sentient, you became something to protect and destroy."

Switzerland is not where I want to go. I know we all have different feelings about returning. Zoe hasn't been there in years. Robbie and I haven't been there in five, or is it six years; since we lost Kara. He wants answers.

On the private jet Zoe has arranged for us, Robbie and she face off. He is trying to remember something and she is soaking up his presence like he is water to her desert. I'm beside him with his arm around me and my head on his shoulder. He leans over and plants a kiss on my head.

"I'll check on Lucy." He stands and stretches then walks to the small bedroom in the rear of the plane.

"So what gives? I need some answers." I say, as she tears her eyes away from him. "Why did you vandalize my apartment and do all those other horrible things? You know him don't you? From before? Is this about jealousy?"

She doesn't answer and just stares at the door where he disappeared. Finally, she closes her eyes. Zoe isn't going to talk, so I leave her and follow Robbie.

He is lying on the bed beside Lucy and moves over so I can slip between them. He wraps himself around me and kisses my neck. "You okay, baby?"

"She won't talk to me. I think she knows you from before. Do you remember?"

"Nah. I get nothing. Some feelings of dread, like I should run or something, you know?"

"She told me at the cabin that all this stuff is happening because the nanites chose me to introduce them to the sentient life. She says there is one group that wants to protect me and one group that wants to destroy me, but that it all revolves around me. I'm the catalyst for everything that is going down."

Thankfully, Lucy stays asleep until we get her situated at the clinic. Dr. Rushing said they have made inroads into working with harmonics and may be able to change Lucy's frequency. She doesn't know how long it will take or if it will revert back to the same frequency. She doesn't really know anything, but we have to try for Lucy's sake.

Robbie wants to know all he can about his TransMEM past, but no one is talking. Zoe practically stalks him, and while she is talking to him, she isn't telling him anything important. She is hoping he will start remembering his time at the clinic on his own. He finds me every chance he can, and has Titan stay with me when he can't.

I'm standing in the hallway when I see Heike walking into the dining room with a small child in tow. She has blonde hair and blue eyes and is skipping and singing, when she notices me and stops. We stare at each other for a few seconds before Heike sees me. Her eyes go wide with fear and she pulls on the child's arm.

"Who is that lady, Heike? Do I know her?" The child asks as she disappears.

I have never seen a child at the spa before, so it must be Heike's little girl. I'll ask her next time I see her. I'm still standing there when Titan makes his presence known.

"She is in the hall by the dining room." He speaks into his phone.

Suddenly, Titan is falling down and an orderly is holding a hypodermic to his throat.

I scream as someone places a cloth over my nose and mouth. The last thing I see is the little girl watching, horrified, as I black out.

CHAPTER 25

Epilogue: ROBBIE

I find Titan right where he said he was, but he is out cold. I can see where a needle was plunged into his neck. Heike runs over and calls for help. A little girl is standing nearby crying. I hold out my hands and she comes to me and throws her arms around my neck. I rub her back and tell her everything will be alright.

"Shhhh. It's okay, darling. Shhhh."

Heike tries to take her from me, but she doesn't want to let go. "No, Heike." She curls her arms tighter around my neck. "I'm staying with my daddy."

"That's not your daddy!"

"Yes it is! We hum!" She looks at me pleading. "Tell her you're my daddy."

I'm trying to take in what this sweet little girl is saying. Hum? Yes, there is a faint hum. "What is your name?" I ask her, looking closer at her features. She has Opal's coloring and my blue eyes and dimples. She is about the right age.

"Kara, Daddy. Don't you know my name?"

Dr. Rushing arrives when Kara tells me her name.

"Jigs up!" I say to her. "You bitch! You kept our daughter from us? You stole her? You put Opal and I through all that grief? You told us she was dead!"

"She is too valuable to be raised by you two." She sneers, hissing and spitting like a damn cat.

"My God! She's our child, not some science experiment. You are going down for this!"

Zoe steps up behind Dr. Rushing and shoves a gun in her back. "Robbie, we have to find Opal and get out of here." She turns and looks down the hall towards our room. "Come closer," she says to the gathering security, "and I'll shoot her!"

"Back away! This is all for nothing if I'm dead."

"Where is Opal, Sylvie?" Zoe asks, shoving the gun harder in the doctor's back.

"In the operating room." She says quietly.

"Let's go." Zoe hands me a gun. "You watch the rear."

I move Kara to my back and tell her we are going for a piggyback ride. She hangs on while I walk behind Zoe backwards. Opal is in the room, laying sound asleep.

"Opal! I shake her a bit. Opal!"

She stirs, but doesn't open her eyes. I notice she has a white gauze patch on her head.

"Too late!" Dr. Rushing laughs like a crazy person. Zoe

knocks her out with the side of her gun. I frown at her.

"What? She's easier to handle now. Here, call your security to get us out of here."

I put in the call. "They will be here in a few minutes. Did you call your people?" I ask.

"Yeah, but we will have to destroy all this information. If we don't, the government will never leave us alone. Do you know how to use a computer?"

"Nope."

Kara is still in my arms and I'm not putting her down. She keeps kissing my cheek and telling me she loves me. What a sweet child!

Heike walks in through Dr. Rushing's private office. "Here, I'll help you Zoe."

"You trust her?" I say, as I turn the gun on her.

"Yeah. Because she is a HuMEM too and she doesn't want to become obsolete, do you, Heike?" Zoe is downloading a virus that will destroy everything on the central computers as well as every individual computer that runs on the spa's website. Heike destroys Dr. Rushing's office files on the computer and all the paper files, which she sets fire to, disabling the sprinklers before she destroys the computer.

"Will this take care of everything?"

"Unfortunately, there is an underground storage site, but I haven't a clue where it is. Sylvie kept it secret and only

Garrett and a few others will know how to find it. But if we don't know where it is, it should be safe from the government as well."

She sighs. "Shit! What a mess!"

"I need to get my men to find Lucy. Didn't she have the last of the harmonic treatments today?" I turn and talk to Titan who has finally appeared, none the worse for wear.

"Grab one of the dudes in scrubs and threaten him if he doesn't take you to Lucy. Get her and bring her to us; and then get a goddamn plane in here to get us out! Set a fire as a distraction."

I look at Zoe. "Wouldn't it be easier just to bomb the place? Level it?"

She laughs at me. "Don't be an ass."

Two hours later, we've loaded everybody onto the plane. Opal and Lucy are unconscious; Zoe and Heike are keeping an eye on the Dragon Lady, while I take care of Kara. I don't know where we should go, but I decide we should head to my family holdings in Scotland. We have a large castle with plenty of underground facilities where we can be safe and monitor things from a distance. We will land on an island and travel by boat, since we don't want anyone finding a plane landing on the property.

"Oh God, where am I?"

Opal is awake and shaking. I wrap a blanket around her

and hug her to my chest. Kara climbs onto my lap and lays her head against her mother. Opal looks confused and passes out again. The hum is sublime with the three of us in contact.

Before we get to shore, Opal wakes again. She stares confusedly at my face, without a sign of recognition.

"What is happening?" She looks at her hands and feels down her body. "Oh God, what is happening?" She panics, but sees Kara asleep on her chest and raises a hand to brush her hair away from her face. "Laura? Sweetie?" she murmurs.

Then I know something is very wrong.

The next installment of The HuMEM Series, imMEMortals, will be available in the fall of 2014.

GLOSSARY OF TERMS

HuMEMs – are humans whose DNA have been used by MEM technology to transform them into superlative humans

imMEMortals – Another name for humans who have gone through the TransMEM and whose bodies are regenerated by the MEMs that have a symbiotic relationship with them.

MEMERGENCE - The emerging of sentientness to the MEMs or NANITES.

MEMs – Microelectromechanical systems is the technology of micromachines at the nano-scale.

NANITES – are machines or devices currently under research and development stage whose components are close to the scale of a nanometer. In the context of this book, they are nano-robots with the ability to read human DNA and regenerate entire bodies.

NANO-SCALE – One nanometer is one-billionth of a meter. A sheet of paper is about 100,000 nanometers thick. A strand of human DNA is 2.5 nanometers in diameter. One nanometer is about as long as your fingernail grows in one second. A human hair is approximately 80,000- 100,000 nanometers wide.

TransMEM – The process of transformation from human to HuMEM.

ACKNOWLEDGEMENTS

First I would like to thank my family and friends for the support and encouragement that you have given to me all these months. I appreciate the faith you have in my abilities to bring this story to paper. I would also like to thank my Editor, Laurel Barlett who struggled through rough weather problems, the flu, and holidays to help me with my manuscript. Thank you readers. I hope you enjoy this first installment of the HuMEM Series. Hat's off to my cover designer, Steven J. Catizone, whose brilliance shows in his art work.

About the Author Kate Donnelly

Although Kate spent 10 years travelling around Europe, she prefers living in the Nashville, TN area where her family is located. She and her husband enjoy travelling out west and camping whenever they can. She has visited Guatemala several times and loves the wild beauty of the unpopulated areas.

Her favorite saying is "What you feed grows and what you starve dies. Make sure you are feeding your imagination."

Facebook: Author Kate Donnelly
WEBSITE: www.authorkatedonnelly.com

Made in the USA
Charleston, SC
13 April 2015